THOROUGHBRED

GLORY IN DANGER

WRITTEN BY
KAREN BENTLEY

CREATED BY
JOANNA CAMPBELL

HarperPaperbacks
A Division of HarperCollins*Publishers*

HarperPaperbacks   *A Division of* HarperCollins*Publishers*
10 East 53rd Street, New York, N.Y. 10022

First printing: July 1996

Printed in the United States of America

HarperPaperbacks and colophon are trademarks of HarperCollins*Publishers*

❖ 10 9 8

For John

Cindy couldn't believe this was happening. . . .

"I should be with Glory," Cindy said, her voice cracking.

"He's all right," Ashleigh told her. "Len is watching him, and we just paged Dr. Smith. She'll get there in a minute. The track vet already examined him."

Cindy tried to think how Glory could have tested positive for a drug, but her mind refused to work. Someone was trying to hurt her beloved horse. "Who would do such a horrible thing?" she cried.

"I don't know," Ashleigh said. "Possibly this is directed at Whitebrook."

"I shouldn't have left him," Cindy said miserably. She could never forgive herself for that. She'd gone off and enjoyed herself while Glory was drugged.

"Cindy, your being here wouldn't have changed anything," Ian said, squeezing her shoulder. "Glory could have gotten the drug anytime during the past two weeks. You can't be on twenty-four-hour guard with him."

"Sounds like a good idea," Cindy murmured. She decided she wasn't going to leave the colt alone one minute more than she had to now. Not when his life was in danger.

Collect all the books in the Thoroughbred series

Collect all the books in the Ashleigh series

*coming soon

GLORY
IN DANGER

1

WHERE IS EVERYBODY? CINDY MCLEAN WONDERED AS SHE walked up the gravel drive to Whitebrook, the Thoroughbred training and breeding farm where she lived. The bus had just dropped her off after school.

At four o'clock on a Tuesday afternoon Cindy expected to see a hubbub of activity around the farm. Usually her dad, Ian McLean, and Len, the barn manager, would be longeing or walking the dozen sleek, fit Thoroughbred horses being readied for races. Ashleigh Griffen and Mike Reese, the co-owners of the farm, often saddled horses in the afternoon to take them on conditioning trail rides. And Vic Taleski, Whitebrook's only full-time groom, should be brushing the horses outside in the warm, early May sunlight.

Instead Cindy saw an utterly deserted stable yard. A puff of dust spiraled in front of the big, two-hundred-year-old red barn where the horses in training were kept. Across the drive stood the beautiful old farmhouse that belonged to Ashleigh, Mike, and Gene Reese, Mike's father, and the McLeans' much smaller, quaint white cottage. Cindy didn't see any signs of life up there, either.

She stopped in her tracks and stared around her, perplexed. *I hope one of the horses isn't sick and everybody's inside one of the barns trying to save it,* she thought.

Suddenly a big grin split Cindy's face. She knew what had happened to everybody. She began to run toward the smaller breeding and foaling barn, next to the training barn.

In the middle of the barn a crowd had gathered. Cindy dumped her backpack in the aisle and hurried to Ashleigh's Wonder's stall.

"Cindy!" Samantha, Cindy's eighteen-year-old sister, was smiling broadly. "We've got a huge surprise for you. Look in there."

Cindy squeezed through the group of adults and looked over the half door to Wonder's stall. Inside was Wonder, Ashleigh's champion mare, winner of the Kentucky Derby and Breeders' Cup Classic. Wonder was standing near the door, looking tired but content. Behind her a small, dark bundle unfolded itself from the straw and stepped shakily around Wonder.

The foal's bright, inquisitive dark eyes looked at Cindy. He had Wonder's markings—four white stockings and a snip at the end of his nose—but he was much darker brown. Cindy's experienced eye noted the little colt's finely molded body and elegantly shaped head.

"He was born an hour ago," Ashleigh said, her hazel eyes sparkling. "Isn't he a beauty?"

"He sure is! Can I go inside the stall and pet him?" Cindy couldn't believe how perfect the foal was. She knew how happy everyone at Whitebrook must be that the colt was alive and healthy. Wonder hadn't had a foal in two years, since Mr. Wonderful. The past year, she had gone into early labor and lost the foal she had been carrying.

"Of course you can go in, Cindy," Ashleigh said. "You've been around enough foals to know what to do."

Cindy eased open the stall door and walked slowly toward the colt. He was watching her fearlessly, bracing himself on his long, slender legs. "Oh, you're such an incredible baby," she said softly, crouching beside him. She ran her hand along his short back, relishing the feel of his thick, fine coat.

The colt looked around and gave her a firm push with his nose. Cindy fell backward into the straw. "Hey, cut it out," she said, laughing.

"He's a strong one," Ashleigh said. "Most foals can hardly stand up right after they're born."

"Wonder outdid herself this time." Mike put his arm around Ashleigh's shoulders.

"I bet this is Wonder's next champ." Ashleigh smiled.

Cindy hoped Wonder's new foal would help make up to Ashleigh for the other disasters that had happened to Wonder and her offspring. First Wonder had broken her cannon bone, ending her racing career. Then Wonder's daughter, Townsend Princess, had broken the same bone when Lavinia Townsend, the daughter of Princess's half-

3

owner, recklessly worked the filly. Just a month earlier Princess had broken her leg again and barely survived. Now Mr. Wonderful, Wonder's two-year-old son, was injured.

"I'm glad we bred Wonder to Townsend Victor this time." Ian frowned. "Wonder's foals with Baldasar have been unsound. Look at Princess, and now Mr. Wonderful. And she lost Baldasar's foal before Mr. Wonderful."

"Dr. Smith doesn't think Mr. Wonderful's injury is career-threatening," Ashleigh argued. "He's strained a tendon, not broken a leg."

"I hope you're right," Ian said.

"Wonder's breeding to Townsend Prince certainly worked out well," Beth McLean reminded them. "Wonder's Pride was Horse of the Year—you can't ask for a more distinguished racing career than he had." Beth was Ian's wife and Cindy's adoptive mother. Beth was an aerobics instructor, but in the year since she had married Ian, she had become almost as much a horseperson as everyone at Whitebrook.

"That's just one of Wonder's offspring, though," Mike said. "And even Pride colicked when he was only four and had to be retired."

"Should be interesting to see what happens with this new little guy," Len remarked, a big smile creasing his weathered face.

The foal was tossing his small head. Cindy couldn't take her eyes off him. "What are you going to name him?" she asked.

"Aren't you responsible for naming the horses around here?" Vic teased.

Cindy realized that was true. Starting over a year before, with Four Leaf Clover and Rainbow, two orphan foals she had helped nurse back to health, she had named almost every new horse on the farm. Back then, Cindy was an orphan herself.

Sometimes those days seemed like a blur to Cindy. She'd been lonely, unhappy, and on the run from a terrible foster home. Now she had everything she'd ever dreamed of: a loving family and a wonderful life on one of the finest Thoroughbred horse farms in Kentucky. Cindy was so involved in every aspect of life at Whitebrook, she felt as if she'd always been there. That included exercise-riding March to Glory, the farm's newest megastar at the track.

Glory! Cindy realized he was probably wondering where she was. She always went straight to his paddock after school. Cindy got up carefully from the straw, moving slowly so as not to startle the baby or mother.

The tiny colt cocked his head. He seemed to wonder where she was going so soon. "I'll come visit you later," Cindy promised. "But right now I've got to ride Glory."

"I suppose we all should get back to work." Ashleigh turned reluctantly from the stall.

"I'll keep an eye on these two for a bit until the vet gets here," Len said. "Dr. Smith's coming, but she just had an emergency call. She's booked up solid almost every day— she's got a lot of clients."

Cindy took a last look at the colt. He was energetically bumping Wonder's flank as he nursed. He certainly was a lively one, she thought. She'd have to think up just the right name for him.

Outside the barn, Cindy squinted in the bright sunshine. She could see Glory grazing at the very back of the big side pasture with two of the older exercise horses. He was so far away, he looked like a small silver cloud on the blue horizon.

Cindy walked over to the gate and removed the colt's halter and lead rope from a fence post. "Glory!" she called.

The gray's head jerked up. He whirled and stood still. Cindy heard a faint snort as Glory sniffed the air.

The next second the big horse was flying. He thundered across the paddock toward Cindy as if a field of racehorses were in full pursuit. His black-and-gray mane and tail streamed behind him as he reached for ground.

Cindy smiled and leaned on the gate. Her heart thumped with pride. "How could anyone have ever doubted that you'd be a great racehorse?" she murmured. In his very first race, a month earlier, Glory had set a track record.

Impressed as she was by Glory's running performance, Cindy was relieved when the colt slowed to a trot as he approached her. After the discussion of unsoundness in the barn, she wasn't in the mood for him to get even a scratch.

Glory slid to a stop in front of her. "Hi, boy!" Cindy ran her hands over the big horse's glossy dappled neck and down his heavily muscled shoulders. "You're the most beautiful, fastest horse ever," she said, hugging him.

For a moment Glory leaned into the caress. Then he shook his head, as if he were remembering something. He briskly nosed Cindy's jeans pockets until he found a carrot.

"Yes, that's for you," Cindy said. "I brought you an extra one, since I'm late."

Glory whinnied indignantly. He eyed her as he crunched the second carrot.

"I know—we need to get some exercise." Cindy buckled on the colt's halter. "You'll be racing again next weekend!" Glory was scheduled to run in an allowance race at Churchill Downs.

Glory charged out of the gate ahead of her.

"Wait up!" Holding Glory's rope in one hand, Cindy tried to latch the gate with the other. Glory tugged vigorously, and Cindy lost her grip on the gate. It swung back and crashed against the fence.

Shining, Samantha's prize red roan racehorse, was watching the struggle from the front paddock, as if she wondered who would win.

"All right, Glory," Cindy said, pulling him closer to the gate. "We *are* going to get this shut and you *are* going to walk up to the barn like a gentleman."

To her surprise Glory stuck out his nose and shoved the gate. They shut it together.

"Thanks," Cindy said with a laugh. "You're a big help."

Glory shook his head. Cindy thought he looked pleased with himself.

"Sammy will be out to get you soon," she called to

Shining as she walked Glory up to the barn. The big mare was hanging her head over the top rail of the fence, obviously hoping to be taken out, too. Cindy knew Samantha was spending a lot of time working with Shining. At the end of May the mare would be running in the prestigious Metropolitan Handicap at the Belmont Park racetrack in New York.

"I can't believe I get out of school a whole week early to help with Shining at the races," Cindy told Glory as she led him into the training barn. "I was really smart when I offered to be Shining's groom last year, even though I didn't know it then. And you'll be going to Belmont, too, if you do well in your next race. But I know you will!"

Glory rubbed his head against her arm. Either he agreed with her or the bugs were getting to him, she decided.

In the barn Cindy quickly tacked up the big gray horse and walked him out into the stable yard. She still didn't see Dr. Smith's truck—the vet hadn't come out yet to look at the new foal.

That meant Max wasn't there, either. Max Smith was in Cindy's sixth-grade class. He often went on rounds with his mother, since he wanted to be a vet, too.

Cindy felt a twinge of disappointment. Then she shrugged and mounted up. "I'll see him in school," she reminded herself as she headed Glory for the woods. Max was fun to be around. For one thing, he was a great rider. And he seemed to be as interested in horses as Cindy was. Glory was one of his favorites.

Cindy leaned forward, pressing her cheek to Glory's

silken mane. "This is a fantastic day for a ride," she said to the colt. A fat red-breasted robin was singing loudly on a fence post, and the thick, brilliant-green leaves of the overhanging trees trembled in the warm breeze. Black-eyed Susans nodded as Glory's hooves brushed them.

Glory stepped lightly along, clearly enjoying himself as much as she was. He looked with interest at the robin and at a large, blue-winged dragonfly spinning its wings in front of them.

The gorgeous, hot late spring weather promised that summer, Cindy's favorite time of year, was close. This year summer also meant the Belmont meet with her family and Mike and Ashleigh—then on to the famous old track at Saratoga near the end of July. Cindy loved the idea of spending all summer in New York with the horses.

She let Glory wander along the path for a while. The colt had such a strenuous training schedule, she thought he was entitled to a little relaxation under saddle sometimes. Cindy was careful not to let her own attention wander, even though Glory had calmed down considerably since the early days of his training.

Before Cindy had known Glory, two men had stolen him from his first owner, then viciously whipped him as a training method. Glory had come to Whitebrook afraid of whips and with bad memories of the track. That all seemed far in the past. Now Glory was a dream to train and exercise-ride.

Cindy leaned back, enjoying the spring in the colt's spirited, energetic walk. As she felt the controlled power of the horse beneath her, Cindy remembered his first race.

Glory had stunned the racing world with his twenty-length win. It would be the first victory of many, Cindy was sure.

She trotted Glory out for about a mile, then turned him toward home. The sun was still bright and high, but soon it would be time for her to help feed the horses. Glory picked up the pace, obviously thinking about his dinner, too.

As Cindy rode into the stable yard she saw Dr. Smith's truck parked in the drive. She wondered again if Max had shown up. *Even if Max isn't here, I can watch Dr. Smith work,* she thought. She liked Dr. Smith, who had a firm but very gentle hand with the horses. She was said to be one of the best vets in the area.

Len met Cindy at the door to the barn. "I'll cool him out if you want to see what Dr. Smith is up to," he said, taking the colt's reins.

"Thanks." Cindy smiled. Everyone at Whitebrook knew she was thinking about becoming a vet. "I'll come see you in just a few minutes, boy," she added to Glory.

In the breeding and foaling barn Dr. Smith was examining Princess's leg. Cindy winced as she watched the slender, dark-haired vet examine the filly's injury.

Princess is so badly hurt, Cindy thought sadly. The filly had broken her right foreleg at the track three weeks before. Princess's injured leg was encased in a cast from her hoof to her shoulder.

Samantha was leaning on a stall door across the aisle to watch Dr. Smith work. Ashleigh stood close to Princess, holding her head and talking softly to her. The beautiful filly seemed to understand. She had put her head in Ashleigh's arms.

Cindy knew that Princess was alive mostly because of Ashleigh's love. Without Ashleigh's constant attention, Princess almost surely wouldn't have tolerated the pain and confinement resulting from her injuries and would have had to be put down.

"Princess is coming along," Dr. Smith said to Ashleigh. "But there's still the danger of infection." Cindy knew that an infection was always possible with a leg as badly lacerated as Princess's. But Dr. Smith was almost certainly referring to what would happen if Princess broke off her cast out of frustration and contaminated her wounds.

Cindy blinked back tears as the vet and Ashleigh eased Princess into her stall. It was hard to believe that Princess could barely walk. Such a short time ago she had been one of the fastest racehorses in the world.

Ashleigh seemed to be thinking the same thing. "The Kentucky Derby is this weekend," she said with a sigh as she shut the stall door.

"I'm sorry, Ashleigh," Samantha said quietly. Princess had been scheduled to run in the Derby until her injury. Cindy knew Ashleigh must be terribly disappointed.

Ashleigh would be riding Glory in his allowance race on Derby day. But Cindy knew that wasn't at all like being Princess's jockey in the Kentucky Derby, the most renowned horse race of the year.

Glory will make everybody at Whitebrook proud, though, Cindy said to herself.

"Let's take a look at Mr. Wonderful." Dr. Smith picked up her medical bag. "How's he doing?"

"He's raring to go," Samantha said. "He seems completely recovered."

"Yeah, he does," Cindy said as they approached Mr. Wonderful's stall. Wonder's handsome younger son had his head over the stall door. Mr. Wonderful was too much of a gentleman to kick the stall or lunge at them from impatience. The chestnut colt merely looked at them indignantly, as if to say, *Aren't you ever going to let me out of here?*

"Are the Townsends giving you trouble about taking him out of training for so long?" Samantha asked Ashleigh.

Cindy scowled at the mention of the Townsends. They owned Townsend Acres, one of the largest Thoroughbred training and breeding farms in Kentucky. Ashleigh and Mr. Townsend each owned half of Wonder and all her offspring—Wonder's Pride, Princess, Mr. Wonderful, and now Wonder's new foal. The arrangement dated back to the days when Ashleigh's parents had been the breeding managers at Townsend Acres. Ashleigh had saved Wonder's life, nursing the weak, sick foal into a champion, and Mr. Townsend had given Ashleigh a half interest in Wonder out of gratitude.

But Ashleigh's dealings with the Townsends had never been smooth. Brad and Lavinia Townsend, Mr. Townsend's son and daughter-in-law, often were careless about the well-being of their horses. It seemed to Cindy that they were only interested in winning races so that they could get big purses and good press coverage. Brad and Lavinia had insisted that Ashleigh run Princess in what turned out to be her last race, dismissing Cindy's concern that something was wrong with Princess's leg.

"I haven't heard a peep out of the Townsends," Ashleigh said to Samantha. "They know how lucky we are that Princess is even alive. I don't think they'll ever pressure me to run an injured horse again."

Dr. Smith put Mr. Wonderful in crossties and carefully ran her hands over his left foreleg. "I don't feel any heat or swelling," she said. "I'd give him at least two more weeks off before you put him back in training, though. He can go out in the paddock, but try to keep him quiet. I know that's difficult with a young Thoroughbred racehorse, but I want to make sure his leg is completely healed. We don't want the tendon to bow."

"What would that do?" Cindy asked.

"The tendon supports Mr. Wonderful's leg bones. A bowed tendon won't do that adequately," Dr. Smith explained. "Once the tendon is bowed, it rarely recovers enough to provide proper support."

"Oh." Cindy gulped. That sounded serious. But she noticed Ashleigh and Samantha were nodding.

"It's just something you have to keep in mind during training," Samantha said.

Dr. Smith looked at Ashleigh. "This isn't the kind of injury that will keep him out of the Triple Crown races next year. But I don't know about the Breeders' Cup in October. We'll have to keep evaluating him."

Cindy planned to race Glory in the Breeders' Cup, too.

She knew it was premature to expect Glory to win a Breeders' Cup race after he had only one victory. But Cindy had always been so sure Glory was fast, she had been planning his Breeders' Cup debut before he raced at all.

It's too bad Max isn't here so I can talk to him about Glory, Cindy thought. Max had faith in Glory, too.

"Where's Max?" Cindy asked Dr. Smith.

Samantha laughed. Cindy glared at her. She knew that her older sister thought Max had a crush on her and vice versa.

"Oh, he's been with the new foal since we got here," Dr. Smith said. "Why don't you go say hi?"

"Okay." Cindy headed for the breeding barn, ignoring Samantha's grin.

Max was sitting on the floor of Wonder's stall, gently patting the foal's side. The baby was flopped flat out, asleep. "Isn't he something?" Max whispered. His green eyes were shining.

"Probably the most beautiful colt I've ever seen." Cindy quietly let herself into the stall. But despite her care the foal woke up. He flicked his oversize ears and immediately struggled to his feet. "Look at that—he didn't fall once," she marveled.

Wonder leaned around and gently pushed her baby toward her flank. But the colt walked over to Cindy, flicking his short tail. Just before he reached her he did a little hop.

"My mom says he's fine," Max said, getting up. "Hey, she said you can go on rounds with us Saturday after next, if you want. I didn't forget I asked you to come. I just wasn't sure when I had to go see my dad in Seattle."

"Great!" Cindy was pleased.

She looked thoughtfully at the exquisite young horse. She was sure he would prove to everyone that Wonder could produce another great winner like Wonder's Pride.

The foal looked up at her and nudged her hand. "I know just what we'll call you," Cindy said. "Wonder's Champion."

2

"I GOT AN INTERESTING PHONE CALL TODAY," BETH SAID TO Cindy from the hallway of the McLeans' cottage.

Cindy had just said good-bye to Max and Wonder's Champion and was on her way up to her room to do homework before dinner. "Who was it?" she asked, turning on the stairs.

"Ben Cavell," Beth said. "Actually his wife, Marie, called. They've invited us to come visit them at their farm in Virginia this summer."

"Wow! That would be super!" Ben Cavell had been Glory's first trainer. Cindy hadn't seen him since just after Glory's first victory at the track, when Ben had looked almost as happy and excited as she was.

"They have a particular reason for wanting you to come now," Beth said, smiling. "A colt out of Ben's Just Victory mare was born just last week. Ben thought you might like to see him."

"Would I ever!" Cindy grinned broadly. She wondered if the new colt would look as much like Just Victory, Glory's grandfather, as Glory did. The great stallion's descendants tended to look like him, although none until Glory seemed to have his speed.

"I think we can squeeze in a visit to the Cavells on our way to Belmont," Beth said. "The third week of May would be convenient for them, too."

Ian walked in from the living room. "That sounds reasonable, as long as we don't stay for more than a day or two. We have to be at the track in New York when the horses get there."

"I wish I could go with you," Samantha said, looking over the banister from the second floor. "I'll still have classes—I'll be lucky if I can get to New York more than a few days before Shining's race."

"I can't wait to see Ben again!" Cindy said eagerly. Ben had given her invaluable training tips about Glory. Somehow he had always appeared out of the blue when she needed him most. It had been Ben who had finally helped Cindy, Samantha, and Ashleigh solve the problem of Glory's fears on the track. All Glory needed, it turned out, was gentle verbal reassurance.

Cindy bounded up the stairs and set her schoolbooks on the desk in her small, neat room. Usually Cindy loved to study there. Beth and Samantha had lovingly painted it rose and decorated it with curtains and a bedspread in floral-print chintz. But now Cindy was too excited even to sit down.

She walked over to her bookshelves. In front of her

veterinary books and books on training was the silver bracelet Ben had given her just before Glory's first race.

Cindy picked it up and rested it in the palm of her hand. As always, the mysterious horses on the bracelet seemed to run, galloping after each other in an endless circle.

Ben promised he'd tell me the story behind this bracelet someday, Cindy thought. *Maybe he will when we visit him.*

"How come you get to go on a great vacation and I'm not going anywhere this summer?" Heather Gilbert complained as she and Cindy walked to their sixth-grade classroom the next morning. "You even get out of school early!"

"I'm just lucky." Cindy shrugged. She hadn't meant to brag to her best friend about all the good news. Cindy knew her summer plans sounded fantastic. "The only bad thing about it is that you won't be along," she added. "I won't know anybody my age in New York."

"But you'll have Glory's and Shining's races to watch and all kinds of exciting things to do," Heather said. "I don't have anything to do all summer except work on my jumping at Tor's and help with the Pony Commandos." Tor Nelson was Samantha's longtime boyfriend. He and his father ran a jumping stable on the outskirts of Lexington. Heather had begun taking jumping lessons there several months earlier.

The Pony Commandos were a group of disabled children who took riding lessons from Tor. Cindy and

Heather helped out with the lessons every Wednesday after school.

"I'm glad you can help with the Commandos, since I'll be gone all summer," Cindy said. "We've got their lesson today."

"Right," Heather answered as they took their seats in the classroom.

"Hey, Cindy," Max greeted her. He and Cindy sat next to each other. "How's Wonder's Champion?"

"Up and at 'em." Cindy smiled, remembering how the feisty colt had greeted her with a loud, strong whinny when she'd come into the stall to feed Wonder that morning. Cindy had wished she didn't have to leave him.

The PA system on the wall crackled. "Cindy McLean, please report to the principal's office," a voice said.

Everyone in the class turned to stare at her. Cindy blushed to the roots of her hair and slouched in her seat. She hated to be the focus of everybody's attention.

"What's that about?" Max asked.

"I have no idea. I didn't do anything wrong," Cindy protested. "I mean, I don't think I did."

"Cindy, you're excused," said Mr. Daniels, their teacher.

"Good luck," Max whispered as Cindy got up.

"Thanks." Cindy's heart was hammering. Heather looked at her questioningly as she passed. Cindy just shrugged.

She hurried down the empty hall to the principal's office. *What does he want?* she thought worriedly. Cindy was afraid of the principal and other figures of authority.

During the long and difficult adoption process, Cindy had feared every day that she would be summoned to the social worker and taken away from Whitebrook. *Nobody can do anything to me now, since I'm legally adopted*, she tried to reassure herself.

The principal, Mr. Eastman, sat with a young man who was scribbling in a notebook. He was wearing jeans and a polo shirt.

Cindy relaxed a little. He didn't look like a social worker.

"Sit down, Cindy," Mr. Eastman said. His plump face was friendly, instead of stern the way it usually was. "This is Mr. George Stryland, from the Lexington *Post*. He'd like to do a human-interest story on you and the racehorse you found, since, as Mr. Stryland has told me, this coming weekend will be the horse's next race."

Cindy let out a sigh of relief. "Sure," she said happily. She knew that Whitebrook could always use good publicity. And nobody had to coax her to talk about Glory.

"So tell me how you got your horse—March to Glory." The reporter looked interested.

Cindy leaned forward eagerly. "I was out riding one day with my friend and we saw him in a field near our farm. He was the most beautiful horse I'd ever seen." Cindy smiled at the memory. Then her face clouded over. "But the next time I rode by, I saw two men whipping him."

"What did you do?" Mr. Stryland looked concerned.

"Not much. Everybody thought I was exaggerating

how badly Glory was being treated, because it's stupid to mistreat a racehorse—a horse won't run well if it's frightened and hurt. And Glory wasn't our horse, so we really couldn't help him. But finally the men hurt Glory so much, he broke out of the field. I found him running loose in the woods and hid him."

Mr. Stryland smiled. "How did you hide a horse?"

"It wasn't easy." Cindy shook her head, remembering how scared she had been that Glory would be discovered and sent back to those awful men. "I put him in an old shed while I tried to figure out what to do. Then I realized that if I showed everybody how fast Glory was, Whitebrook, our farm, would want to buy him. So my sister, Samantha, rode him on the track." Cindy didn't add that she'd tried to work Glory first—and he'd almost thrown her. She hadn't known a lot about horses back then. "Whitebrook kind of adopted Glory while we looked for his real owner," she added.

"You're adopted, too, aren't you?" the reporter said gently.

"Yes." Cindy didn't mind if people knew that.

"Whitebrook bought Glory at the Keeneland auction in January, right?" Mr. Stryland went on.

"That's right—we found Glory's real owner, who wanted to sell him. Then Glory set a track record in his first race."

"And the thieves went to jail," Mr. Stryland said.

Cindy nodded. "They got a long sentence."

"Prison's tough these days," the reporter remarked.

"Well, those men were really cruel to Glory," Cindy

21

said. "My parents said the judge wouldn't have been so hard on the thieves if they'd only stolen Glory and not mistreated him."

Mr. Stryland made a few more notes. "That should cover it," he said. "Thanks a lot, Cindy. This will be in Thursday's paper."

Cindy shook hands with the reporter and ran to her gym class. She was almost laughing with relief. She hadn't gotten in trouble—she was practically famous!

The huge, cavernous gym echoed with the sounds of bouncing volleyballs and the shouts of students. Cindy sat on a bleacher to watch. Class was almost finished, and she wasn't anxious to play volleyball anyway.

Max walked over from one of the games, twirling a volleyball on his finger. "So what happened?" he asked. "Did you get detention?"

"No—a reporter wanted to interview me about Glory," Cindy said proudly.

"How come?" Max looked impressed.

"Because Glory's racing again this weekend." Cindy smiled. She could hardly wait.

"Yeah, you told me." Max looked wistful. "I wish I could see the race, but I'll be in Seattle. Good luck."

"I don't think we'll need luck," Cindy said confidently. "Glory's so fast, he'll win against even top-class allowance horses. He's going to be a stakes winner, too—I'm sure of it."

3

"WALK, EVERYBODY!" TOR CALLED. HE STOOD AT THE center of the big indoor ring at the Nelsons' stable, frowning with concentration as he watched the Pony Commandos warm up.

The five boys and girls in the class began their lesson, helped by Cindy, Heather, Tor, and Samantha. Cindy walked beside Jane McKendrick.

"Watch this!" Jane rose in the stirrups, carefully balancing over Milk Dud's neck. The bay pony obligingly slowed his walk.

"Super, Jane," Cindy cheered. That might not be such an incredible trick for the average kid, Cindy thought, but Jane had been born with severely deformed legs. She was confined to a wheelchair.

"I want to do that at a trot next," Jane confided. "Then maybe I can jump like Mandy."

Cindy smiled at the eager, dark-haired little girl.

"Maybe you can!" she said. Mandy Jarvis was the star of the Pony Commandos. Eight-year-old Mandy had started out as a Commando, but through hard work and sheer force of personality she had learned to ride so well that Tor gave her private lessons now. Mandy's dream was to ride in the Olympics.

Tor's a great teacher, Cindy thought. *Maybe the reason Mandy won't need her leg braces soon is that she got so much stronger and her balance improved so much here.* Since the Commandos had started the lessons, a year and a half before, all of them had improved not only physically but also mentally. Everyone in the class loved to ride.

"Okay, let's watch Aaron jump for a few minutes while the rest of you catch your breath," Tor said. Aaron Fineberg was the only Commando who jumped now that Mandy was gone.

Aaron effortlessly took his short spotted pony, Speckles, over two low crossbars and a foot-high parallel. Cindy applauded enthusiastically. A second later she heard someone echoing her applause.

"Look, there's Mandy!" Jane said.

Cindy turned. Mandy stood at the entrance to the ring, holding the reins of her pony, Butterball, and clapping. The trim eight-year-old, her legs still encased in heavy metal braces, would have her private lesson with Tor after the Commandos' lesson. "Way to go, Aaron," she yelled.

Right behind Mandy was a tall, handsome man. He walked with her into the ring.

"Who's that?" Heather whispered, coming up behind

Cindy with Charmaine Green and Zorro, a gentle black pony.

"Rory Griffen, Ashleigh's little brother." Cindy knew Rory from one or two get-togethers at Ashleigh's parents' farm. She saw that Samantha and Tor were looking at Rory, too.

Heather giggled. "He's not very little."

"No, Ashleigh said he'll start college this fall. He's been away at private school for a long time."

"Sammy!" Rory called.

"Rory! You're back!" Samantha ran across the ring and hugged him.

Tor finished guiding Aaron through the jumps and walked over to Samantha and Rory.

"Rory, this is Tor," Samantha said. "He owns the stable with his father. Tor, this is Ashleigh's brother, Rory." The two men shook hands cordially.

"Why are we just standing here? Can't we do something?" Jane complained to Cindy. Milk Dud stamped his small hoof, as if he was tired of waiting as well.

"Just a sec. Wait till Tor tells us what to do." Cindy was curious about why Rory had come to the stable.

"What brings you to town?" Tor asked Rory.

"I'm home for the summer. I thought I'd come over and see if you needed a hand. I know Beth couldn't make it today." Rory looked around the ring with interest.

"Fantastic." Samantha beamed. "If you can take over for me, I'll go tack up Sierra and get ready to work him. Don't worry," she said to Tor. "Rory knows everything about horses—he's been riding since he was five."

"Good." Tor frowned slightly. Cindy wondered if Rory knew more about horses than Tor did.

Rory walked to the side of the ring and grabbed Milk Dud and Zorro's bridles. "Two at once!" he shouted, leading off Jane and Charmaine. All the Commandos giggled.

Rory walked beside Jane and Charmaine as they practiced figure eights. "Tighten up on your inside rein," he said to Jane. "But don't turn the pony—"

"His name's Milk Dud," Jane told Rory.

"Don't turn Milk Dud too sharply or you'll lose your balance. Like this." Rory took Milk Dud's left rein and gradually turned him. "Now you try."

Jane carefully turned the pony. In a few minutes she was trotting a figure eight.

Cindy noticed that Rory seemed to know just when to give encouragement and support to Jane without doing everything for her. *He's great with the kids,* Cindy thought.

"Thanks, Rory," Tor said at the end of the Commandos' lesson. "You helped a lot."

At that moment Samantha rode Sierra into the ring. The big liver chestnut was playing with the bit and rolling his eyes back to look at Samantha. Cindy knew that Sierra might be the most promising steeplechaser in the world, but he was also a holy terror.

Samantha stayed completely unruffled as Sierra jerked his head, trying to get more rein, and crabstepped. She looked wonderful riding the spirited horse.

"I think I'll stick around for a bit and watch Mandy and Samantha," Rory said.

"We can sit on the bleachers over there." Cindy pointed to the side of the ring.

"I'll help Jane put up Milk Dud," Heather said. Cindy knew that the other Commandos could lead their horses out of the ring by themselves.

Rory and Cindy walked over to the bleachers and sat in the front row. "I heard from Ashleigh that you're a great exercise rider, Cindy," Rory said.

"Thanks!" Nothing pleased Cindy more than to hear that the talented young trainer thought well of her.

Mandy and Samantha circled the ring at a canter. Then Samantha warmed up Sierra over a couple of three-foot parallels and oxers. Sierra leaped the substantial jumps as if they were cavalletti.

"Let's make it a little more challenging," Tor said. While Samantha circled Sierra, he raised some of the jumps to four feet and some to four and a half.

Sierra sailed over the first jump, a four-foot oxer more than two feet across. Samantha's hands were low on Sierra's neck. Her back was straight and her heels were down. For a moment Cindy imagined the blissful sensation of flying that Samantha must feel riding over such a big jump.

Sierra gracefully found his feet again on the landing. Samantha sat back, and they cantered on. Cindy realized that Sierra wasn't the only one whose jumping form had improved—Samantha looked like a pro.

Rory whistled. "Not bad, huh?" Samantha called. "This monster's really coming into his own."

Samantha jumped Sierra over the challenging course

27

Tor had set up, consisting of two four-foot parallels, a broad oxer, a water jump, and a large brush jump. Sierra's ears were pricked, and his eyes were bright and interested. Cindy could hardly believe this horse had lazed his way along the flat racetrack and had nearly been sold.

"I'm going to take off after I cool him out," Samantha said to Tor, pulling up Sierra in front of him. She took off her helmet and shook out her red hair. "How about if I van Sierra over to Whitebrook this week? That way I can start working him outside."

Tor nodded. "Fine—but I'll miss you." Cindy knew that Sierra spent only winters at the Nelsons' stable. Once the weather warmed up, he could be worked on the outside turf track at Whitebrook. Samantha had kept Sierra at Tor's this long to make it easier for Tor to fit coaching her into his busy schedule.

Sierra's ears pricked. Suddenly he snaked out his head and grabbed a mouthful of Tor's shirtsleeve.

"Sierra!" Tor cried, easing his shirt out of the big horse's mouth.

Sierra jerked his head away. His eyes had a devilish gleam, Cindy thought.

Samantha laughed. "You'll miss me, Tor, but you won't miss him."

Tor grimaced. "Not around the barn, anyway. We can't let him out for a minute by himself—I don't think there's any fence he can't jump. I guess I should be glad, though. That's true on the steeplechase courses as well."

"I'll give you a ride home," Rory offered Samantha.

"Thanks!" Samantha smiled. "We can talk over old

times. Just let me put up Sierra. By that time Mandy's lesson will be over, and Cindy will be ready to go, too. Okay, Cindy?"

"Sure," Cindy said. She was anxious to get back to Glory and Wonder's Champion. Rory followed Samantha into the barn to hear more about Sierra.

Tor walked back out to the center of the ring. Mandy was trotting Butterball around the ring, posting. "Hey, Mandy! Get those heels down and your legs under you!" Tor called. "You look like you're spurring a bucking bronc!"

Cindy winced. She was sure Tor didn't mean to sound so critical, but she thought he should go easier on Mandy. Although Mandy's legs were stronger these days, she still couldn't grip with them as well as the average kid. And Mandy took criticism very hard. As the little girl rode by, Cindy saw tears in her dark eyes.

"Ready to try some jumps?" Tor asked.

"Sure," Mandy said determinedly.

"Warm up on these two crossbars." Tor adjusted the rails on one of the jumps to form a low X. "Then we'll try a two-and-a-half-foot parallel today."

Cindy smiled, leaning back on the bleacher behind her. Mandy had never jumped anything over two feet. Tor must be pleased with her progress.

Butterball cleared the two low jumps.

"Okay!" Tor clapped briskly. "Now I want you to take the two and a half footer. Then circle back around the ring and take the crossbars again."

Mandy headed the caramel-colored pony for the higher parallel that Tor had set up in the center of the ring. Cindy

29

held her breath. She saw Samantha walk back into the ring and stand near the doorway to watch.

Mandy cued Butterball with her legs, and the small pony gathered himself alertly for the jump. Butterball always put his whole heart into every jump, Cindy thought.

Mandy flew over the rail with the pony, eyes ahead, already looking to the next jump. She completed the course perfectly.

"Nice, Mandy!" Tor called. "Let's call it a day and put Butterball up. Good job."

Mandy nodded and rode Butterball to the side of the ring. Cindy tried to catch her eye to congratulate her. But Mandy was staring straight ahead, looking dazed.

I wonder what's wrong, Cindy thought. *Maybe she's just tired.*

Samantha seemed to have noticed the same thing. She walked toward Tor. "Do you think you're pressuring Mandy too much?" she asked.

"What do you mean?" Tor asked in surprise. "Mandy did great over those jumps. I don't think there's any limit to what she can do."

I'm not sure about that, Cindy thought with a worried frown. *Mandy looks exhausted. I just hope she can keep going at this pace.*

The next morning Cindy only walked Glory, taking him several times around the track. The colt's race was in just two days, and that was all the exercise Ian, Glory's official trainer, and Ashleigh wanted to give him. After Cindy had brushed Glory and put him in his stall, she headed to the breeding barn. Len had asked her to put Wonder and Wonder's Champion out in one of the small paddocks for the day. They'd been out the previous day for the first time.

"Ready to see the world some more, little guy?" Cindy asked the foal as she slipped a halter over Wonder's head.

Wonder's Champion gave a snort and moved right to the stall door. He wasn't a bit shy, Cindy thought. He seemed to know just how important he was already.

Wonder walked quietly out to the paddock with her foal frisking at her heels. Cindy released the mare onto the luxuriant grass and leaned for a moment on the fence, watching her tear up big mouthfuls of the fresh, tasty food. "That really does look good, Wonder," she said, opening the gate to join them.

Wonder's Champion cantered across the field, stretching out his long legs. The colt seemed to enjoy the feel of his supple, agile body.

"You already like to run fast, don't you?" Cindy called. His name definitely suited him, she thought.

She flopped down on the grass, relishing its damp coolness on her hands. The clouds, high streaks of white, looked brushed onto the pale blue sky. It was going to be a beautiful day. Cindy was sorry she'd have to spend it in school.

"Cindy!" Beth called from the house.

Cindy jerked out of her daydream. *School!* She jumped

up and rushed for the gate. It would be a miracle if she didn't miss the bus.

Wonder's Champion ran toward the gate with her, his strides easy and floating. He seemed to think Cindy had invented a new game for them to play.

"No, you can't go to school, baby, even though that would be fun. I'll see you later," Cindy said, quickly closing the gate before he could get out. Wonder's Champion watched her go, his small ears pricked. He obviously was puzzled by Cindy's sudden flurry of activity.

Cindy burst into the McLeans' cottage and hurriedly poured a bowl of cereal in the kitchen. She estimated that she had a minute and forty-five seconds before the school bus stopped at the foot of the drive to pick her up.

It's going to be close, she thought, grabbing her backpack.

Beth and Ian walked into the kitchen, smiling. "Did you see today's paper?" Beth asked Cindy.

Cindy shook her head, swallowing a last bite of cereal.

"'Girl and Horse March to Glory,'" Beth read. "Not a bad headline."

"Oh, the article on Glory came out!" Cindy grinned.

Ian handed it to her to read. "Don't let your head get too big," he cautioned.

Cindy quickly scanned the article. The reporter had said great things about her and Glory. "The epic story of a girl and her horse," he had begun the article. Cindy tried not to feel smug as she read, but it was hard.

"I can say I knew you when," Samantha said as she

rushed through the kitchen, grabbing an apple from the fruit bowl. She shut the front door with a bang. A second later her car roared.

Startled, Cindy looked up. "I'm sure I missed the bus!" she said. "It's really late."

"I'll drive you to school," Beth said with a laugh. "You're a celebrity—you shouldn't have to take an ordinary old bus, at least for one day."

When Cindy got to school, Max, Heather, and several of the other kids in Cindy's class were standing in front of her locker, reading the newspaper.

"Hey, it's the famous horsewoman," Max said.

Cindy blushed. "Thanks! I couldn't believe all the stuff that guy said."

"Your mom and dad must be proud," Heather said.

"They are." Cindy couldn't help looking pleased with herself.

During first period Mr. Daniels read the article out loud to the class. Cindy blushed the whole time, but she was happy too. *I think I like being famous,* she thought. *And it's only going to get better when Glory's a champion.*

4

"COME ON, GLORY!" CINDY PUSHED HER BLOND HAIR OUT OF
her face. A cool wind was blowing as she led Glory to his
stall on the backside of Churchill Downs. In just an hour
the colt would run for the second time, in a seven-furlong
allowance race.

Cindy had noticed that horses always knew when it
was race day. Probably that was because they weren't fed
as much in the morning, and they also picked up on the
tension in the air. She had been walking Glory around the
shed row to keep him from getting nervous, but the big
horse seemed fine. In fact, Cindy was having trouble
getting him to move along, because he wanted to stop and
socialize with the other horses.

Tens of thousands of people crowded the famous track
that day, Derby day. On the backside elegant
Thoroughbreds, blanketed in their stable colors, stepped
lightly after their grooms. Even though Glory wasn't

running in a major race, Cindy felt the electricity running through the backside on the day of the Kentucky Derby, the first leg of the Triple Crown.

Glory tugged on the rope, trying to touch the inquiring nose of a chestnut somebody had just led up to them. Cindy reacted quickly to pull Glory away.

"Control your horse," said an angry voice.

Cindy looked around Glory and saw Brad Townsend, his handsome face set in a scowl. He was jerking on the lead line of the horse Glory had been trying to nuzzle.

Oh, no, she thought. *Why did I have to run into him?* Behind Brad she saw Lavinia, holding their new baby, Lawrence Hotchkiss-Ross Townsend, or Ross for short. Ashleigh had received a birth announcement two weeks earlier. Since the Townsends didn't care much for Ashleigh, Cindy could only assume they'd sent announcements to the entire world. Lavinia was wearing a sheer flowered silk dress, and the baby wore a matching blue silk shorts outfit. The expression on Lavinia's face was even more unpleasant than Brad's.

The Townsends didn't have a Derby entry this year, either, after Princess's injury. Cindy imagined that was adding to their bad mood.

She pulled Glory even farther from their horse. Glory wasn't acting up. It was really Brad who was causing trouble, not the horses, she thought. She wondered what Brad could be thinking of anyway, bringing another colt this close to Glory. Colts were notorious for fighting with each other and for their unpredictable moods.

"So you're running him again today?" Brad asked, jerking a thumb in Glory's direction.

"Yes, in an allowance race." Cindy kept a good grip on Glory's lead just to make sure he stayed where he was. But the gray horse was standing quietly, sniffing in Lavinia's direction. He probably didn't know what to make of her perfume.

"I guess he's up to it," Brad said. He was examining Glory closely.

"Of course he is!" Cindy said angrily. "You saw how he did in his first race!"

"Any horse can win *one* race against a field of maidens." Brad shrugged.

Cindy decided to shut up. She was just going to get in over her head, arguing with the Townsends. Brad would see for himself, very soon, what Glory could do.

Suddenly Cindy remembered what Ben Cavell had said right before Glory's first race, when he had rescued her from Brad's taunts. Ben had said that Brad knew exactly what Glory was capable of and wanted to keep an eye on him. Cindy smiled.

Lavinia's baby began to cry. Lavinia glared at Cindy as if it were her fault. "Come on, Brad," she said. "We've certainly seen enough here. The Alexanders are expecting us."

Cindy watched them walk off through the crowd. The Alexanders, she knew, owned the Kentucky Derby favorite, Salutation.

She looked back at Glory. He was lightly tugging on the lead line to remind her that he was waiting. "That's right, boy—forget about them. You've got a race to run," she said. Her stomach fluttered with excitement just at the thought of it.

Cindy put Glory in crossties and ran a brush over his sleek shoulder. The shed row was quiet and peaceful. Glory must be the only horse stabled there who was running in the allowance race, Cindy thought. Sunlight streamed through the open barn door, glinting off Glory's silvery dappled coat.

"Brad always times it just right to catch me alone," Cindy said. "I guess he thinks I can't stick up for you, Glory. But I can. I'd rather die than let the Townsends have anything to do with you."

Cindy had heard through the grapevine that Lavinia wasn't in any trouble with her father over what had happened to Princess. The reason was her baby, Ross Townsend. Mr. Townsend was said to be thrilled with his new grandson.

"Lavinia always manages to get away with murder," Cindy muttered.

Glory turned to look at her. There was so much affection and trust in his gaze that Cindy's heart melted. "I'll always take good care of you. I promise," she said.

Cindy wiped down Glory's coat with a finishing cloth, stroking it smoothly over his highly toned muscles. She stepped back to examine her work.

Mike, Len, and her dad walked up. "All set?" Mike asked.

"Almost." Cindy decided not to mention the Townsends' visit. Mike would just be angered by their interfering. He couldn't stand the way they treated Ashleigh.

Cindy had one more thing to do before Glory was

ready to go to the saddling paddock. She took the big horse's head in her hands. "Listen, boy," she said softly.

Glory obligingly stepped forward. Cindy cradled his head in her arms. "Go out there and win," she said. "No funny business. No spooking or daydreaming. This is important."

Glory rubbed his ear against her shirt. He seemed to be saying, *Fine by me.*

Cindy had to force herself to walk calmly as she and Len led the stallion to the saddling paddock. The sharp wind whipped Glory's mane, and Cindy heard occasional cries as the ladies' traditional broad-brimmed hats lifted off into the air. Cindy felt like jumping into the air herself.

"Glory won his first race on a windy day like this," she said to Len. "Maybe it's his favorite kind of day. I know he's going to win again!"

"I think you just may be right," Len agreed, running a hand down Glory's neck.

Ashleigh was waiting at the saddling paddock, wearing the blue-and-white silks of Whitebrook. Most of the horses in the race were still in the paddock stalls, being saddled by their trainers and grooms. A few circled the paddock at a walk.

Len quickly placed Glory's saddle pad on his back and fastened the featherlight racing saddle. Glory stood calmly, like an old pro.

"I think I'm as relaxed as he is," Ashleigh said. "This is my only ride for the day."

"Do you mind not riding in the Derby?" Cindy asked.

She knew that Ashleigh had been offered two mounts in the race, but she had turned them down.

Ashleigh shook her head. "The Derby is always an extremely challenging race. I decided I don't want to ride so hard right now after all," she said. "There's always next year, with Mr. Wonderful."

Cindy guessed Ashleigh really didn't want to ride any horse in this year's Derby but Princess. *She must be taking Princess's injury harder than anyone suspects*, Cindy thought. But it was fine with Cindy if Ashleigh wanted to spend all her time on Glory.

Ashleigh mounted up and gathered Glory's reins. "The competition's pretty stiff in this race," she said. "No one's afraid of Glory yet—they're not trying to avoid going up against him. He ran a great race last time, but that was only one race."

"They'll be afraid of him soon." Cindy grinned. She was sure of that.

"I think so." Ashleigh frowned.

Cindy wondered why Ashleigh was being so cautious. Glory had put in a stunning work at the track five days before. Cindy looked up at Ashleigh. "Well, good luck."

"Thanks." Ashleigh smiled a million-dollar smile that made Cindy long fiercely to be like her—a brilliant young jockey and successful trainer, about to ride professionally in a race.

Someday I'll ride out there, Cindy thought as she walked to the stands to join the Whitebrook group. *I just have to be patient and learn everything I can.*

"The track's fast," Samantha commented as Cindy sat down next to her.

"Maybe Glory will set another track record." Cindy picked up her binoculars and focused them. The horses were just coming out onto the track for the post parade.

"He's the one-to-five favorite," Mike said. "But some trainers think it's bad luck to go off as the favorite."

"Do you?" Cindy asked. Ashleigh had just ridden Glory onto the track. The magnificent horse stood poised for several seconds, ears pricked as he looked at the freshly harrowed track, the seven other horses in the field, and the people packed into the stands and infield. Cindy was glad to see that even a sudden swarm of Frisbees flying across the infield scarcely made Glory blink.

The noise from the crowd swelled as Ashleigh put the stallion into a canter going clockwise.

"I don't think it's bad luck for him to be the favorite today," Mike said with a laugh.

"They're cheering him on," Beth added. "That article in the paper about you two, Cindy, has really elevated Glory to star status."

Cindy smiled proudly. At school on Thursday a dozen kids had come up to her and wanted to know more about Glory's racing career.

"I don't mean to burst anybody's balloon, but I think Flightful's going to give Glory a run for his money," Ian said, leaning around Beth.

Cindy moved her binoculars to Flightful, the number-four horse. Flightful's jockey was heading him toward the starting gate on the backstretch. The colt was a blocky, muscular black, and the jockey had him on a tight rein. Flightful's head was down and his powerful neck arched as he tried to get more rein. He did look like a real contender, Cindy thought.

"He's as small as a pony," Samantha said. "He can't be more than fifteen hands—maybe fifteen-two."

"His breeding's not much, either," Mike noted.

"Whatever Flightful's flaws, somehow he won his first two races going away," Ian said.

"Yeah, but with these horses just beginning to race, that doesn't mean much. Flightful could be a nine days' wonder," Mike answered.

Cindy felt a tremor of nervousness. That was what Brad Townsend, and even Ashleigh, had said about Glory. But it couldn't be true in Glory's case.

Cindy watched as the horses were loaded in the gate. For once they all went in quietly, without balking or other trouble. The starting bell clanged loudly in the sudden stillness.

"And they're off!" the announcer shouted.

Glory broke sharply from the gate and angled in along the rail. "Good, good," Cindy muttered, clenching her hands. Usually the horse on the rail had an advantage, since it had the shortest distance to run. Glory continued to pull away from the pack, his strides fluid and effortless.

Suddenly Flightful shot up beside Glory. The black colt pounded along Glory's flank. "Looks like an early speed duel between March to Glory and Flightful!" the announcer called.

Cindy saw Ashleigh glance back, then let Glory out a

41

notch. The two front-runners swept around the first turn, already five lengths ahead of the rest of the field. But Flightful wasn't giving up an inch. He stayed right at Glory's flank. Then he began to draw even.

"No! Go, Glory!" Cindy screamed. "Don't let him catch you!"

Ian put a steadying hand on her shoulder. "Take it easy," he shouted over the noise of the crowd. "Glory's got a lot more to give!"

Her dad was right, Cindy saw as she frantically gripped the rail in front of her. At the quarter pole Ashleigh, or maybe Glory, decided to put away the competition. Suddenly Glory wasn't just running—he was a blur of speed and energy. He powered around the final turn, switched leads, and bounded down the stretch for the wire.

Now Cindy could hear Glory's hoofbeats, like rapidly approaching thunder. He was going unbelievably fast— she could tell that without looking at the fractions on the board. He had speed to burn!

Flightful dropped back a length, then two lengths. The rest of the horses in the field were so far back, Cindy thought they looked as though they were in another race. "Win it, boy!" she screeched. "You're wonderful!"

Glory flew under the wire. Ashleigh stood in her stirrups, signaling him to slow. Glory tossed his head and broke into a canter, then a high-stepping trot. Even from this distance Cindy could tell that the race hadn't taken much out of him.

He's absolutely incredible, she thought. *This is like a dream!*

"And Flightful comes up short in the stretch run," the announcer called. "Most impressive about this race is that March to Glory was never asked for anything!"

"I think that horse is ready to go the classic distance," Mike said. "He was still pouring on speed at the end." He grinned at Cindy. "I guess Glory wasn't a bad buy after all."

Cindy grinned back. For a while, when Glory's training had been going badly, Mike had been one of Glory's biggest doubters. First he had thought Glory wouldn't run at all, then he didn't think he could go the classic distance of a mile and a quarter. That had certainly changed.

"Let's get out there to the winner's circle!" Beth said briskly.

Ashleigh was just riding Glory up when they arrived. The press were already shouting out questions to her. "How do you explain Glory's explosive finish?" asked a reporter from one of the major racing papers.

"I asked Glory to run in the stretch and he responded very strongly," Ashleigh said, dismounting to weigh in with the saddle.

Cindy took hold of Glory's bridle. He was barely blowing, and his shiny neck had only traces of sweat. "Thanks, big guy!" Cindy said happily.

"He really looks like a champion," one of the reporters said thoughtfully. "He's got the powerful quarters and long-muscled shoulders of one."

"Let's get our champ cooled out," Ashleigh said to Cindy.

"We'll meet you back in the stands," Ian said.

As she and Ashleigh walked Glory through the tunnel

to the backside, Cindy heard the echo of a horse's hooves behind them. Turning, she saw Flightful with his jockey and trainer. The black horse was still blowing hard.

"Good race," the jockey called to Ashleigh.

"Thanks, Felipe," Ashleigh said.

"This race was a disappointment," the trainer said. "Of course, with the track bias, what could we expect?"

"Right, Joe." Ashleigh began walking a little faster.

"But your horse still went like he had wings," Joe continued.

Somehow Cindy didn't think Glory was getting a compliment.

The trainer hurried after Ashleigh. "So how did you do it?"

Ashleigh sighed wearily. "Work and breeding, I suppose."

"Great training," Cindy added loyally.

"Really," Joe said. "Well, Ashleigh, I suppose you're referring to the fact that Flightful has fairly humble breeding. But he's a very game horse. He ran an honest race today, without any drugs, which seem to be so prevalent in some circles of racing these days. A lot of people wanted Flightful to win."

"Of course," Ashleigh said politely. "Now if you'll excuse me, I've got to see to Glory." Ashleigh turned toward the Whitebrook shed row.

"Glory's just a perfect horse," Cindy said to Ashleigh when they were alone. "That's why he won."

"It's no surprise to me." Ashleigh shrugged. "He won his first race by twenty lengths. So the track was favoring the rail today. All the other jockeys knew that, too—

Glory's race wasn't the first on the card, and it was obvious that every other horse that ran on the rail today had an advantage. Flightful was outfinished—Joe's lucky his horse got up for second against ours. The only surprise was that Flightful stayed up with Glory at all."

"*I* think so," Cindy said proudly.

"Well, I'm done for today." Ashleigh yawned. "Wow, I'm tired!"

"I'll sponge Glory and cool him out," Cindy said. She couldn't wait to be alone with the colt so that she could tell him again and again how wonderful he was.

"I think I'll go get a cup of tea." Ashleigh yawned again.

"That was a fantastic ride, Ashleigh," Cindy said shyly. "Thanks."

"No thanks necessary." Ashleigh smiled warmly.

Cindy put Glory in crossties and gave him a lukewarm sponge bath. The colt loved water. He closed his eyes blissfully, relishing the gentle strokes of the sponge across his back and flanks.

Cindy hugged her damp horse. "I guess I should be thanking *you*, Glory," she said. "For everything you've done for me and Whitebrook—and everything you're going to do."

5

THE NEXT SATURDAY, SAMANTHA DROPPED CINDY OFF AT THE Smiths' farm so that Cindy could go with Dr. Smith and Max on veterinary rounds.

"Have fun," Samantha said, smiling.

"I will." Cindy shut the car door. She wished Samantha would stop looking at her like that. She knew her older sister thought she had a date with Max.

Cindy walked up the drive toward the Smiths' modern ranch-style house. She stopped for a moment to enjoy the smell of the grass hay growing in a nearby field, warmed by the bright yellow sun.

These days Cindy felt as though she was enjoying everything. The past week, after Glory's victory in his allowance race, had been the best in her life. Most of the kids at school had been at Churchill Downs on Derby day, and practically everyone had congratulated her on Glory's big win. She smiled to herself.

A small herd of horses was grazing in a large, grassy paddock to her right. Cindy climbed up on the lowest board of the fence to look at them. They weren't all Thoroughbreds, she realized. Two were paints and one was a palomino—Thoroughbreds didn't come in those colors. And the horses had the muscular, bulky builds of Quarter Horses.

They were gorgeous—and powerful sprinters, Cindy knew. Quarter Horses could run a quarter mile faster than any breed of horse in the world.

"Hey, you got here," Max said from behind her.

Cindy turned. The sunlight glinted in Max's dark hair. He wore jeans and a dark green T-shirt that matched his eyes. *He's definitely the cutest boy in my class,* Cindy thought.

Suddenly she felt a little shy. "Hi," she said. "How come you've got so many Quarter Horses? I thought you said your mother reconditions horses from the track."

"She does. Some of those guys are from the Quarter Horse tracks. My mom's reconditioning them for barrel racing and other Western timed events."

Cindy stretched out her hand to the white muzzle of a curious paint who had wandered over to the fence. The horse had beautiful big patches of brown and white that looked like maps and a black-and-white mane and tail. The horse lipped at her hand, apparently hoping for a treat.

"Guess what," Max said. "I just found out that my mom and I are going to Belmont, too. Some of her bigger clients want her along to keep an eye on their horses."

47

"That's fantastic!" Cindy grinned. She'd have a friend to share all the excitement of Glory's next race—and to explore New York with. *Now I'm sure the summer's going to be perfect,* she thought.

"Yeah, isn't it?" Max smiled back at her and looked up toward the house. "My mom's about ready to go," he said. "She's loading the truck with her instruments and supplies."

"Okay." Cindy jumped off the fence and followed Max up the drive. Dr. Smith was checking the medicine chest in the back of the truck. Next to her stood a slender young man.

"Hi, Cindy," she said. "This is Jim Trewell, my new assistant. I'm so glad I finally got some help. I was barely getting to my emergency calls on time."

Cindy and Jim shook hands. "Pleased to meet you," she said.

Jim nodded. Cindy noticed that although he was smiling at her, his eyes were cold. *Maybe he thinks I'm just a dumb kid who'll get in the way,* she thought.

"Let's get started," Dr. Smith said. Cindy and Max climbed into the backseat of Dr. Smith's big pickup.

Cindy looked out the window as they drove through the countryside. Young foals, that year's crop, filled the white-fenced paddocks. Some were frolicking with other foals, while others flicked their little tails as they walked behind their mothers. A few nursed quietly.

Cindy smiled, thinking of Wonder's Champion. Everybody at Whitebrook had loved the name. The hardy foal was already boss of the other four foals he and Wonder were pastured with, even though he was at least a month younger than they were.

"Our first visit is a lame horse," Dr. Smith said as they drove toward Lexington. "The horse has been coming up lame off and on for several months."

Cindy leaned forward. "Why?"

"I don't know yet," Dr. Smith said. "This is a racehorse. Because of the symptoms I can rule out a few causes of the lameness. It can't be caused by an abscess, for example, because that would cause acute, steady pain. The on-and-off pain the horse is suffering might be from joint disease, bone chips, or any number of things. I've never treated this horse before, so I don't have much of an idea."

"Dynamite had an abscess, but he's fine now," Max said, referring to his own Thoroughbred. Max turned to Cindy. "Let's ride together."

Cindy grinned. "Are you saying that you want to race me and Glory?"

"How about if we ride at my place?" Max said quickly. "I'll ride Dynamite, and you can ride some old paint."

Cindy laughed. "I saw some pretty good horses in your paddock. I think I'll pick a good one."

She turned to look out the window again. To her surprise, she saw that they were pulling into the Alexanders' luxurious estate. Salutation, the Alexanders' horse, had gone on to win the Kentucky Derby the past Saturday. *Maybe we'll see him!* Cindy thought.

The thick, deep green grass of the acres of lawn was shaded by ancient oaks. A high, vine-covered privacy fence surrounded the house. Behind the house Cindy could see at least five red-painted barns.

This place is even bigger and more impressive than Townsend Acres, she thought.

Dr. Smith parked in front of one of the barns. An elderly man walked quickly out to the truck. "I'm Reg Salisbury, head trainer. Glad you could make it—the horse is lame again."

Dr. Smith gathered her medical bag and what looked to Cindy like a pair of big iron tweezers. "Where is he?" she asked.

"Out back," Salisbury said. "Mrs. Alexander's letting him graze a little."

In the alley between two of the barns a magnificent chestnut was tearing up big mouthfuls of grass, as if he knew the treat wouldn't last long. When he saw Dr. Smith he stopped grazing and stared, as if to say, *I know exactly who you are—and I don't think I like it.*

Cindy gasped. There was no mistaking the broad blaze, finely crested neck, and elegant, slender legs of the Kentucky Derby winner. "Isn't that Salutation?" she asked.

"Yes, it is." Dr. Smith walked over to the colt. A petite middle-aged blond woman held Salutation's lead rope. She was talking softly to him.

"I'm Grace Alexander," the woman said, extending her hand to Dr. Smith. Cindy noticed that Mrs. Alexander was dressed as beautifully as Lavinia Townsend, in a long, flowing flowered silk dress that seemed a bit out of place in a stable. But unlike Lavinia, her smile was warm and genuine.

"How do you do," Dr. Smith said. "Please bring him into the barn—we can get a better look there."

"Come on, sweetheart," Mrs. Alexander murmured. The big horse walked slowly forward.

Cindy put her hand to her mouth to stifle a gasp. Salutation was limping badly. She couldn't tell what foot he was limping on, but he obviously didn't want to move at all.

Mrs. Alexander led the colt to the barn, talking to him. Salutation walked haltingly behind her. Clearly he was trying to please her, although it was hurting him. Cindy could tell they loved each other very much.

In the spotless barn Mr. Alexander stepped forward and introduced himself and two grooms. He was wearing a business suit and exuded the same sense of wealth and power that Brad's father, Mr. Townsend, did, but Cindy didn't feel nearly as nervous around him. "Let's hope the news is good," he said.

Dr. Smith nodded, but Cindy could see that her mind was already on the problem at hand.

Jim took Salutation's lead line from Mrs. Alexander. "Twitch him?" he asked Dr. Smith. Cindy knew that a twitch was a severe restraint applied to a horse's mouth.

"See how he does without." Dr. Smith ran her hands up and down one of the chestnut colt's forelegs. "No heat or swelling," she said, picking up Salutation's hoof. "Hand me my testers."

Jim handed her the big iron pincers. Dr. Smith moved them across the hoof, squeezing them at intervals.

Cindy held her breath. She knew that any kind of lameness in a racehorse could be career-threatening. And a lot was at stake here. Salutation was entered to run in the

Preakness, the second jewel of the Triple Crown, in just two weeks.

Salutation stood quietly until Dr. Smith reached the back of his hoof. The colt gave a shrill cry of pain and half reared, striking out with his forelegs.

Dr. Smith moved deftly out of range of his hooves. "Steady him," she said tersely to Jim.

Mrs. Alexander stepped forward, reaching for Salutation's halter. "Hush, baby," she whispered. "We're just trying to help." The colt dropped back to his feet, lifting first one forefoot and then the other as he tried to take weight off them. He was still breathing hard, but he allowed Dr. Smith to pick up his other front foot.

She repeated the procedure with the hoof testers, going directly to the back of his foot. This time the colt merely let out a grunt of pain when she squeezed the sore area. Dr. Smith gently replaced his foot on the ground. "It's in both forefeet," she said with a sigh. "I'll have to take radiographs to rule out fractures of the coffin bones, but I think it's navicular."

"Oh, no!" cried Mrs. Alexander.

"The intensive training and then the Derby probably set it off." Dr. Smith frowned.

"Can't you give him some medicine?" Cindy asked. "A couple of horses have come up lame at Whitebrook, but you could always help them."

Jim scowled. Cindy wondered if he thought children shouldn't ask questions.

"I can try giving Salutation isoxsuprine tablets," Dr. Smith said. "It's a vasodilator that will increase blood flow to the hoof. But navicular is a degenerative disease. The navicular bone in the foot has deteriorated, and it almost always progresses. When the pain gets bad enough . . ." She shook her head. "I'm sorry. He's probably still got several good years to stand at stud or as a pleasure horse. I can put him on butamine—a nonsteroidal anti-inflammatory drug—for the pain."

"Don't worry, big guy." Mrs. Alexander had tears in her eyes as she stroked her horse's glossy neck. "So we'll put you out in the paddock instead of running you. We'll take such good care of you."

Dr. Smith gave Salutation his first isoxsuprine tablet and a shot of butamine. Then she issued the Alexanders a supply of the drugs so that they could treat him. The grooms and Mr. Alexander seemed to be in shock, Cindy thought as she walked back to the truck.

But even though Salutation's diagnosis was bad, Cindy was glad Mrs. Alexander seemed to love the colt just as much as before. Cindy was sure he would have a good life for as long as it lasted. Mrs. Alexander didn't care if he couldn't run in the Preakness or the other big races. She just wanted to be with her horse. That was how Cindy felt about Glory.

"Okay, the next case should be straightforward," Dr. Smith said. She rolled her shoulders, as if to ease the tension. "We're going to see a pony that cut itself on a barbed-wire fence. But it's not bad."

"Good," Cindy said. She didn't think she was ready for another case as heart-wrenching as the end of Salutation's racing career.

Dr. Smith stopped the truck in front of a modest house in a new development. Out back in a small paddock was a gentle-looking big pony. A boy about seven was holding his lead rope. The paddock was all dirt, Cindy noticed, but perfectly clean.

"Hi," the boy said. "I'm Sam. Are you the vet?"

"Yes," Dr. Smith said with a reassuring smile. "Is this our patient?"

The little boy nodded. "My mom and dad are at work. They told me to show you Candy's leg."

Dr. Smith climbed over the fence and dropped down next to the pony. He was watching her steadily. "It's okay, Candy," Sam said.

Cindy saw a long cut on the pony's left hind leg. The blood was congealed on it—it was an old wound. It didn't look too serious.

Dr. Smith felt Candy's leg above and below the wound. "He's got a nasty scratch," she said. "The leg is a little warm—it seems to be slightly infected."

She sat back on her heels. "Here's what we'll do, Sam. I'll give him a penicillin shot for the infection. Then I'll give you a salve to put on the cut every day. That will disinfect it and keep the flies away. Think you can do that?"

"Sure," Sam replied seriously. "Candy's my best friend."

Jim went to get the medications from the truck. "Penicillin's a safe, easy treatment for infection," Dr. Smith said to Cindy and Max. "But with racehorses I have to be extremely careful not to give it within two weeks of when the horse will race. Penicillin is injected with procaine, a local anesthetic that numbs the surrounding muscle. Procaine is banned at the track because it also acts as a stimulant."

She handed Sam the salve Jim had brought. "Thanks for saving my pony," Sam said shyly.

"You're welcome." Dr. Smith smiled. "See you, Sam."

Cindy looked back as they walked to the truck. Sam was hugging his pony's neck.

"Nice to be a hero," Dr. Smith said with a chuckle as she and Jim put away the medical supplies. "That was easy." Her mobile phone rang. She switched it on, and her expression became somber as she listened. "Change of plan," she said. "One of the horses I've been treating for colic is down again."

"Is this an emergency?" Cindy asked as the vet tossed the last of her equipment in the back of the truck and ran around to the cab.

"Colic is always an emergency," Dr. Smith said grimly, throwing the truck in gear and pulling quickly back onto the main road.

Cindy remembered Ashleigh's stories about the time Wonder's Pride had colicked, ending his racing career. He had almost died. It had taken him months to recover after surgery.

"Darn," Dr. Smith muttered. "I thought we might have the problem licked with this mare. But she's so old . . . "

"How old?" Max asked.

"Thirty." Dr. Smith smiled slightly. "She's a tough old girl to make it this long. I was hoping she'd pull through."

"What causes colic?" Cindy asked.

"Sometimes you know, and sometimes you don't," Dr. Smith said. "It can be caused by too much rich feed—for example, freshly cut hay, especially if the horse isn't used to it. Moldy hay is another cause."

"The design of the horse's digestive system makes them especially prone to colic," Jim added. "They have very long intestines, even compared to ours, with a lot of loops and narrow areas. It's easy for part of the intestine to become twisted or blocked."

"In an old horse like this, her intestine could just be worn out." Dr. Smith stopped the truck in front of a small, tin-roofed barn, pleasantly shaded by elms. "There's no cure for that."

The horse was up again but standing very still in front of the barn. Occasionally she nosed her flank. As they approached, Cindy could see that the mare was very old. Her back sagged, and the hollows were prominent in her face and below her ears. The owner, a woman in her thirties, was pulling on the lead rope, trying to get the horse to move.

"This is Judy Getz," Dr. Smith introduced them. "What's the latest with Alice?" she asked, gently patting the old horse's neck.

Judy's face looked drawn and tired. "I gave her the banamine injection and bute paste at three this morning," she said. "But her feet seem to be hurting her more. Then I came out a little while ago and she was down."

"Poor old girl." Dr. Smith placed the metal end of her stethoscope against the mare's side. "I don't hear any gut sounds," she said. "That's bad news."

Tears filled Judy's eyes. Cindy rubbed the old horse's nose. The mare was being so brave about her pain.

"What's her name?" Max asked.

"Alice. Silly name, right?" Judy laughed, wiping away her tears with one hand. "But I never got around to changing it. And now she's thirty. I guess she'll be Alice till the day she dies."

Dr. Smith frowned. "The colic's not resolving," she said.

"Can't you do surgery?" Cindy asked. "That helped Pride."

"No, not on a horse as old as this one," Dr. Smith said. "The stress of the anesthetic and the operation would almost certainly kill her. And we've got a new problem that developed a couple of days ago. The soreness in her feet is laminitis—that's swelling of the foot after trauma, in this case the colic. In the worst cases the pressure causes the coffin bone in the hoof to rotate down until the horse is standing on bare bone. It's very painful."

"What are we going to do?" Judy asked sadly.

"It's up to you," Dr. Smith said. "We've been battling this for ten days now. We can continue to try to treat Alice . . . or we can put her down with a quick shot of sodium pentobarbital."

Tears ran down Judy's cheeks. "This is so hard," she choked out.

"It might be for the best," Jim said consolingly. "She's suffered a lot."

"I know." Judy closed her eyes. "All right—I'll let her go."

"You don't have to stay, Judy," Dr. Smith said quietly. "We can take it from here."

"I can't leave her to die alone." Judy sighed. "Not after everything we've been through. We've been together twenty-six years. I got her when I was twelve."

When she was my age, Cindy thought. She glanced at Max. He looked sad and upset, as if he was thinking the same thing.

"Alice won't feel any pain," Dr. Smith said. "The drug's very quick. But it might be better for you not to watch."

Judy nodded slowly. "Just let me say good-bye." She spoke with an effort. "Alice?" she asked.

The old mare turned her head. Her dark eyes were clouded with pain, but her ears pricked at the sound of Judy's familiar voice.

Judy pulled Alice's head to hers and touched her face to her horse's muzzle. "Good, good girl," she said. "I love you so much—forever, and that's a promise. But I have to let you go."

Alice stood quietly, flicking her ears as she listened to the beloved voice of the person she had known for so long.

"Thanks," Judy said to Dr. Smith. "I think I'll go for a walk." Dr. Smith nodded.

After giving Alice a final pat, Judy walked into a grassy, flower-filled paddock behind her house. Cindy wondered if she and Alice had memories together of that place.

Dr. Smith readied the shot.

"I'll hold Alice," Cindy said.

"Are you sure?" Dr. Smith asked. "Jim could hold her. I know this is upsetting."

"I'm okay." Cindy could see that this was a special mare. She wanted to give her all the comfort she could.

58

She leaned near to the mare and rubbed her forehead. Alice didn't smell like a horse. She smelled antiseptic, like medicine.

Cindy looked into the old horse's eyes. Alice waited calmly. Her expression was distant. *She's in so much pain,* Cindy thought. *I don't think she'll mind.*

Dr. Smith walked over, carrying the hypodermic. "Be careful to stand clear, Cindy," she said. "She'll go down fast." Cindy nodded.

Dr. Smith injected the mare in her neck. In a second she dropped to the ground.

"She's gone. A truck will come for her in half an hour," Dr. Smith said. She was looking down at the horse, an expression of pity on her face. "I'm glad Judy left. She wouldn't want to remember her horse like this."

"Poor Judy," Cindy said. She couldn't even imagine how much she would love Glory after twenty-six years with him, when he was almost thirty. By that time she'd be thirty-eight. They'd be almost the same age.

"In some ways Alice isn't really gone," Dr. Smith said. "Judy will always remember her. And the mare had a long, happy life. Judy said she was jumping her over big brush jumps just last week."

"Yeah, but Judy won't feel great coming out to an empty paddock," Max said.

"I know." Dr. Smith sighed. "Sometimes you can cure them; sometimes the best you can do is just manage the pain. And sometimes the kindest thing you can do is end their life," she added quietly. "Well, let's get going. We've got several more stops scheduled."

After three more calls Dr. Smith turned the truck toward Whitebrook. "I want to check Mr. Wonderful's leg one last time," she said. "And we'll drop you off, Cindy."

Cindy leaned her head against the back of the seat. The sun was setting in a soft pastel blend of pink, yellow, and orange. The lush grass waved in the empty paddocks—by now all the horses were in for the night. Cindy was ready to go home.

"I don't know how your mom can stand to do this every day," she said to Max.

"It's hard," Max agreed. "A lot of times when she gets home, she chills out by watching our horses for a while— she says it does her good to see horses that are well. If she doesn't get called to another emergency, that is. She's on call every other night."

Cindy tried to imagine what that would be like. It would be hard work—just as hard as all the preparation and training needed to be a jockey, another career she was considering. But being a vet was rewarding, too. Cindy remembered that Dr. Smith had relieved pain and given comfort everywhere she went.

At Whitebrook, Dr. Smith rewrapped Mr. Wonderful's leg and gave him a final pat. "That should take care of him until tomorrow," she said. "Ashleigh and Len know what to do. I'll be back to check him in a couple of days."

Cindy walked with Max and Dr. Smith out to their truck. "Thanks for letting me come along today," she said shyly.

"We were glad to have you." Dr. Smith smiled. "You're welcome to join us anytime."

"I'd like to go with you again," Cindy replied.

Dr. Smith looked at her watch. "Jim!" she called. "Where are you?"

A moment later Jim emerged from the training barn. "Sorry," he said. "I thought we'd left one of the medical bags back there."

Cindy looked at him in surprise. *I'm almost sure he had both bags in his hands when we all left the barn,* she thought.

"Mandy, no!" Tor rubbed his forehead in frustration. "That's not right at all." Mandy was circling Butterball at a trot the next Wednesday afternoon. It was near the end of Mandy's hour-long private lesson.

I'm glad the lesson is almost over, Cindy thought as she watched from the bleachers. *And I'll bet Mandy is, too.* Mandy wasn't riding as well as she usually did. Even during the flat work her leg position was off, and her hands kept jerking up. Tor hadn't stopped criticizing her the entire time.

Cindy shifted uneasily in her seat. She and Heather exchanged glances. Cindy knew that Tor had a jumping show coming up in a week. He'd be riding High Caliber, a relatively inexperienced jumper. He was also keeping Sierra on a full schedule of steeplechases.

That was a lot of pressure. It might explain why Tor didn't seem to see that he was pushing Mandy so hard.

"All right, let's try three feet," Tor said to Mandy, walking over to one of the jumps. He raised the bar. Then he set up another jump directly behind it to make an oxer.

Cindy raised her eyebrows. Not only would Mandy have to take Butterball over the highest jump she'd ever tried, but she'd have to go across a two-foot width as well. With a pony as small as Butterball, Cindy knew, that wouldn't allow much margin for error. And this wasn't one of Mandy's better days.

Mandy had stopped Butterball and was sitting at the far end of the ring, examining her knee.

"Hey, are you awake out there?" Tor called.

"Yes!" Mandy slid her foot back into the stirrup.

"Take just the one jump," Tor said. "We'll work on your form as Butterball's more extended over the oxer."

Mandy nodded. She gathered her reins and sat quietly for a moment, looking at the jump.

"I hope Tor doesn't keep after me like that in my lesson," Heather whispered. "He's going to work with me later."

"Yeah, he's giving Mandy a tough time."

Mandy put Butterball into a canter and headed him toward the jump. She had him exactly centered on it. Cindy could see that her small face was set with determination.

Butterball's ears pricked forward. The gallant little pony seemed to be concentrating as hard as Mandy was. He lifted, then was up and over. His small hooves hit the ground in a puff of dust.

Perfect jump. Mandy's such a pro, Cindy thought

admiringly. Mandy was patting Butterball's neck and praising him.

"No comment on that one, Mandy," Tor said. "Couldn't be better. Let's end there for today."

Mandy gave a quick, relieved smile. Then she walked Butterball to the side of the ring.

"Come on, Sammy—let's get going with Sierra!" Tor called.

"I want to find Mandy," Cindy said to Heather. "We should tell her that was a super jump."

"I'd better tack up Sasha," Heather said, referring to the small, sweet-tempered mare she rode in her jumping lessons. "I don't want to keep Tor waiting."

Cindy walked down the stable aisle toward Butterball's stall. To her surprise she saw the pony's tack flung in the middle of the aisle. There was no sign of Butterball or Mandy.

Puzzled, Cindy peered into the pony's stall. Mandy was huddled in a corner, crying. Butterball was affectionately nuzzling her.

"Mandy, what's the matter?" Cindy said. "That last jump was perfect. Tor thought so, too."

"I know." Mandy buried her face in Butterball's caramel-colored mane.

"So what's the matter?" Cindy pressed.

"Nothing," Mandy sobbed. "I'll be all right in a second."

"You don't look like nothing's wrong," Cindy said, opening the stall door. She sat down beside Mandy. "What is it?"

Mandy burst into a fresh storm of tears. "I don't want

anyone to give me special treatment," she choked out. "But my legs hurt so much. When we work that hard, the braces rub my skin off."

"Really off?" Cindy was stunned.

Mandy nodded. Gingerly she reached under one of her braces and rolled up her riding breeches a little.

Cindy gasped. Mandy hadn't been exaggerating. The skin on her leg had been rubbed raw, leaving an open, bleeding wound an inch across. Cindy saw the beginning of another one just above the first. Mandy had tried to stick Band-Aids on the blisters, but the bits of plastic were peeling off. "How many of those blisters have you got?" she asked.

"I know exactly." Mandy managed a small smile. "Eight, four on each side. But don't worry—this one is the biggest."

Cindy was horrified. "How can you ride like that?"

"I just make myself believe it doesn't hurt. But that doesn't work after the lesson." Mandy grimaced and carefully rolled her pant leg back down. "I'd better get these breeches in the wash before my mother sees the blood," she added.

"I'm going to tell Tor," Cindy said. She was sure he would immediately cut back on the work he had Mandy do. He would never want her to suffer like this.

"Don't!" Mandy awkwardly jumped to her feet. The effort caused the metal of her braces to rub her open blisters again, and she gasped with pain. "I want Tor to push me," she said through gritted teeth. "I want to ride on the Olympic team."

"You can't ride on the Olympic team if you get blisters like that," Cindy said gently.

"They'll heal," Mandy insisted. "I'll figure out something. Right now I've got to brush Butterball."

"Let me do it," Cindy said quickly. "Just this once."

Mandy smiled through her tears. "Okay—thanks. My dad's probably waiting in the car for me. I'd better get washed up." She slowly limped toward the bathroom.

Heather looked in the stall. She was leading Sasha. "Where's Mandy?" she asked.

"Washing up. Her legs are one big blister," Cindy said.

"How awful!" Heather gasped.

"Yeah, I know. She won't let me tell Tor."

"You'd better anyway," Heather said.

"I would, but the problem is that Mandy wants Tor to keep working her this hard."

"He wouldn't if he knew she was hurt," Heather said firmly.

"Yeah, I don't think so, either."

Mandy looked in the stall. She was carrying Butterball's tack. "Bye, Butter," she said lovingly to her pony. "You were a wonderful boy today. Thanks a lot for helping me, Cindy."

"No problem." Mandy had washed her face, and her old look of determination was back. Cindy couldn't even tell that her friend had been crying.

Mandy's going to hate me if I say anything to Tor, Cindy thought. *I have to let her handle this.* "I'm going to New York next week," she said. "But make sure you write me and tell me what happens with your lessons. I'll give you my address."

"Okay." Mandy grinned. "I might have great news. Who knows how high I'll be jumping by the time you get back?"

6

CINDY LOVED BEN CAVELL'S FARM, SHADOW MAPLES, THE moment she saw it. The Cavells lived in an old white colonial house with massive pillars out front, surrounded by broad green lawns. The thick branches of ancient, gnarled trees hung over the drive.

Getting to Virginia from Kentucky hadn't been easy, at least for her parents, Cindy thought. For the past week Ian and Beth had packed and unpacked and worried about what they might be forgetting that they'd need at the Belmont track. Cindy hadn't had that problem. In just an hour she had her own suitcase ready to go and sitting by the door. Cindy figured all she needed for the next few weeks were jeans and a couple of Belmont T-shirts, which she planned to buy at the track.

The moment the McLeans had arrived at Shadow Maples, Cindy asked to see Glory's half-brother. Ben seemed just as anxious to show her the new colt. He and

Cindy walked around the back of the house to the paddocks while Ben's wife, Marie, escorted Ian and Beth to the shady veranda for a cool drink.

The heat was pretty intense, Cindy thought, brushing damp strands of blond hair off her forehead as she followed Ben. But she couldn't wait another second to see the colt.

"My family has lived at Shadow Maples for generations, since before the Civil War," Ben said as they crossed the backyard.

"Wow!" The farm looked that old, Cindy thought. The grounds were a little overgrown. The orange, white, and yellow roses growing against the house bloomed brilliantly in untidy rows. The wood boards around the paddocks were a soft, weathered gray.

In a small paddock just ahead Cindy saw several sleek horses standing under a tree, switching their tails. Two foals, a black and a gray, frolicked in the sun, seemingly unaware of the heat.

"It's nice to come back to the farm and relax," Ben said, opening the gate to the paddock. "I spend most of the year on the road, since I don't train my own horses. These broodmares are the only horses I own right now."

"Why don't you train here?" Cindy asked. The black foal had walked back over to his mother and was playfully butting her shoulder. But the gray foal was standing very still, watching Cindy. Cindy thought the foal was absolutely gorgeous.

"I'd train my own horses if I had the money," Ben said. "You know how much it costs to run Whitebrook. But

68

someday I hope to have a breeding and training farm here again, the way my great-grandfather did."

"Is that the colt out of the Just Victory mare?" Cindy asked, pointing to the gray.

"Yes. Nice-looking little fellow, isn't he?"

"He sure is." The foal was only a few weeks old, but Cindy could hardly believe how muscular he was already. His finely shaped, elegant head was very much like Glory's.

The foal walked over to Cindy. He sniffed her hands, then moved his muzzle up along her shoulder to her cheek. "He's giving me a kiss!" Cindy laughed, tickling the gray velvet of the foal's nose.

"Just Deserts has taken to you," Ben remarked.

Cindy smiled as she rubbed the colt's star. She wished she could see Glory and Just Deserts together so that she could make some more comparisons.

The bracelet Ben had given Cindy flashed in the sun, as silver as the colt's coat. Cindy shook it back on her wrist.

"That bracelet belonged to my great-grandfather," Ben said. "He ran some of the first Thoroughbreds in this country. But in the war my family lost everything except the land."

"Why did you give the bracelet to me?" Cindy asked shyly.

"Because you deserve it." Ben looked at Cindy thoughtfully. "So does Glory. I see in him the return of Just Victory's greatness."

"Really?" Cindy said excitedly. "That's what I think, too, but nobody else does. I mean, Ashleigh and Mike and my dad think Glory's first two races were fantastic, but they don't—"

"Think he's going down in the history books," Ben finished. "Well, prove them wrong."

Cindy smiled. "I'll try," she said. It was nice to hear a vote of total support for Glory. Cindy had never lacked confidence in her horse, but almost everyone around her seemed to, at least sometimes. She got tired of hearing that Glory was fast *but* he might burn out, he might get hurt, or something else might go wrong.

Ben wiped his forehead. "Let's go back up to the house. Are you ready for some lunch?"

"I sure am." Cindy gave Just Deserts a final pat and followed Ben back across the yard.

"Did you enjoy your tour?" Beth called from the veranda.

"Yes, it was great!" Cindy almost laughed. Beth and Ian were sitting in deep, cushioned wicker chairs, sipping iced drinks. They looked as though they hadn't moved since she and Ben went for their walk.

Cindy had to admit the veranda did look cool and comfortable. It was broad and shaded by leafy old maples. A breeze stirred, rocking a striped hammock.

Marie pushed open the screen door with one hand. She was carrying a tray with the other. "Anybody hungry?" she asked.

"I am!" Cindy said.

"Let me help you with that," Ian said to Marie, standing. He carried the tray of cold cuts and homemade whole-grain bread to a table and set it down. Beth

70

brought out another tray of sliced cantaloupe and watermelon. Finally Ben appeared with two tall pitchers of iced tea and lemonade. The chilled pitchers dripped condensation.

Cindy settled on the porch swing and took a long drink of the sweet, icy cold lemonade Marie poured her. Then Cindy fixed herself a triple-decker turkey, lettuce, and tomato sandwich.

"Eat up," Ben encouraged.

"It's so nice to have you here, Cindy," Marie said. "We have a grown son but no grandchildren—yet. It's been a long time since we had a young person around."

"It's nice to be here," Cindy said. Looking across the porch through the shimmering haze, she could see Just Deserts galloping across the field, oblivious to the heat. Apparently he couldn't wait to run. *Boy, does this beat school,* Cindy thought, filling a bowl with succulent cantaloupe. She smiled to herself. *I hope Heather and Max aren't studying too hard.*

Ben looked out at Just Deserts, too. "He's going to be a joy to train," he remarked. "As I told Cindy, Glory is the best horse I've trained so far. This year I've had a couple of good minor stakes horses and two horses I'm pointing toward major races this summer and fall. But none of them compares to Glory."

Ian raised an eyebrow. "I'm surprised you're so optimistic about him, Ben. I'm Glory's trainer, but even to me Glory really has yet to prove himself. So far, he's won only his maiden and an allowance race. He's never been in stakes company."

"That's true," Ben allowed. "But I like the way he looked in his first two wins." He winked at Cindy. "Sometimes you're willing to stick your neck out about a horse."

Cindy grinned back. She was certainly willing to for Glory.

"I don't mean to sound pessimistic," Ian said. "It's just that you never know what will happen in horse racing. But I'd put my money on him, too." Ian smiled encouragingly at Cindy.

"I'll look for him at Saratoga," Ben said. "I'll be racing a few horses there."

"The van taking Glory and the other horses to Belmont will get to the track tomorrow." Cindy frowned. "I wish I were with him—he must wonder where I am."

"Ashleigh and Mike are traveling with him," Ian reminded her. "He knows them well. Cindy, honey, you have to remember that Glory isn't a pet—he's a racehorse with a job to do. You can't be with him every second. You don't need to coddle him."

Cindy nodded reluctantly. She supposed that was true.

"Glory will have most of the comforts of home at the track," Beth said, sweeping crumbs from her lap. "We'll be there late tomorrow. And Ashleigh will exercise-ride him."

"I wish I could do that," Cindy said.

Ian shook his head. "Cindy, you're too young. It's probably a mistake that I even let you work Glory at home. The Belmont track is completely unfamiliar territory to him, and it will be crowded with other riders."

Cindy frowned. *At least I'll be around for Glory's race,* she consoled herself. Her dad might be right that Glory had to learn to do without coddling, but deep in her heart Cindy didn't think the colt would run his best without her.

"Get out of my way!" Ian honked the horn of the McLeans' rental car on Monday as they drove through the streets of New York City. He yanked the wheel to the right to pass a lumbering delivery truck.

"Ian, try to calm down," Beth said. "We won't get to the track any faster by yelling."

"You're the one who suggested we drive through Manhattan," Ian reminded her.

"I thought it would be fun for Cindy to get her first look at the city," Beth protested.

"It is!" Cindy leaned back to stare out the window at the skyscrapers towering above her. The buildings were so high, the streets were already in shadow at two in the afternoon. New York was by far the biggest, most crowded place she'd ever seen. Along Madison Avenue she saw dozens of store windows stocked with elegant clothes and exotic merchandise. Tourists in bright shirts and businesspeople in conservative suits were drinking cappuccino and eating pastries at sidewalk cafés.

Cindy slipped sideways in the seat as the car lurched into another lane. *Dad's turning into a maniac,* she thought. Beth glanced back at Cindy and rolled her eyes. Cindy grinned and looked out the window again. Now

73

they were in Soho, the artists' district. Her dad turned left toward Long Island.

"There, we're through the city," Ian said, sounding relieved as they coasted over a long bridge. "It's not far to the track now."

Cindy smiled. She couldn't wait to see Belmont Park, home of the Belmont Stakes, the third jewel of the Triple Crown. That year the Breeders' Cup would be held there as well. But best of all, Glory would be waiting for her!

Cindy jumped out of the car the second her dad stopped it in the track parking lot. For a second she wasn't sure where to go. Then she saw Len and Mike standing in front of one of the long shed rows, waving.

Cindy ran toward them, waving back. A trickle of sweat ran down her cheek. If anything, New York was even hotter than Virginia. She didn't care—all that mattered was getting to Glory as soon as possible.

"Hi, Cindy," Len greeted her. "He's inside."

Cindy hurried into the barn, squinting in the dim light. "Glory?" she called.

Glory whinnied imperiously from the center of the barn. Now Cindy could see the big horse's crested neck and finely molded head. She rushed over to the colt and hugged him. "Oh, Glory! I missed you—we've never been away from each other before! Are you all right?"

"Of course he is," Len said from behind her. He shook his head and smiled. "He's been eating like a champ and he's as full of himself as ever. Don't you worry."

Cindy buried her face in her horse's satiny neck. Len was right—Glory was loved and well cared for by everyone around him. She didn't need to worry about him. It was just a bad habit of hers from the early days, right after he had been stolen. Glory nuzzled her again and again, as if he couldn't quite believe she was really there.

"How did he do on the trip?" Ian asked Mike.

"Fine—he handled it like an old pro," Mike answered.

"Ben Cavell, Glory's first trainer, used to feed him in the trailer sometimes," Cindy said. "Then Ben took Glory for drives to get him completely used to it."

Glory tossed his head emphatically. "You're saying that's right, aren't you, big fellow?" Len asked.

Cindy leaned against the colt. It was so good to be back with him. His warm gray coat was like silk against her fingers. When she pressed her cheek to his neck, he smelled like a clean, healthy horse.

"You seem to have done fine on that long road trip," she said. "Now we just have to see how you do tomorrow when you run."

7

Cindy stared out at the track the next morning, her heart pounding. Even at six thirty the air was already thick with humidity, and a burning red sun was rising slowly through the mist. Ashleigh had just ridden Glory onto the track for his first work at Belmont.

"Come on, Glory," Cindy murmured. "This one really counts."

"He looks fit and ready to go," Ian remarked. He and Mike stood beside Cindy at the rail. After Glory's work both men would stay to watch Matchless and Sagebrush, two other Whitebrook horses entered in allowance races that week. Shining had the day off—she would only be walked. Her race was in six days.

"He sure does look ready," Cindy murmured. Glory definitely couldn't look more gorgeous. He was trotting quickly along the track with sure steps, bowing his neck as he asked for more rein. Ashleigh kept him well in hand.

She had to, Cindy realized. The track was crowded with riders and horses, and their movements had to be carefully orchestrated. A high-speed collision of horses could easily be fatal to all involved.

The horses that had been worked earliest were already being walked back to the barns. Horses that had just arrived at the oval were warming up, cantering or trotting clockwise, to the outside of the track.

Close to the rail a horse thundered by, his hooves kicking up the soft dirt, the jockey crouched low over his neck, asking for speed. Cindy knew that riders doing works would have notified the official clocker to time them.

"Glad we were with the early set," one of the exercise riders commented as he guided his horse through the gap in the oval.

"Yeah, this heat is a killer," answered his companion.

"Hey, Dad, that one rider was about my age," Cindy said to her father.

"I doubt it," Ian said. "Most riders are small—he was probably in his twenties. I know what you're thinking, Cindy, but don't. You can't exercise-ride at a major track until you're at least sixteen."

Cindy sighed and looked out at the track. Ashleigh was fully focused on Glory as they rounded the far turn, headed for the three-eighths pole.

"Here comes Glory," Mike said tensely. "Ashleigh's starting his work."

At first Cindy couldn't see Glory behind a group of horses walking on the track. Then suddenly he burst clear.

One of the slow-moving horses gave a frightened whinny and tried to bolt. The rider quickly pulled him up. Cindy squinted into the sun, watching her magnificent horse in action.

Glory roared down the stretch. To Cindy, he didn't seem fully extended—he just seemed to be going for an easy gallop. But then she saw the massive thrust of his muscled shoulders and hindquarters at every stride. The track slipped away behind him effortlessly. How could he run so fast? Cindy thought in wonder.

Several of the riders had stopped their horses to watch. Glory glided past the finish—and kept going.

"He's really on fire!" Samantha said admiringly.

"I hope Ashleigh can pull him up." Ian frowned.

"Never a doubt," Mike answered.

Cindy saw that Ashleigh had made Glory drop back into a canter, then a trot. Posting, she trotted Glory back around to the gap. The gray stallion was blowing a little, but his eyes were bright and interested. The work seemed to have inspired him instead of calmed him down.

"Now that's a black-type work," Ian said with satisfaction, glancing at his stopwatch.

Cindy grinned. Horses earned black type in the daily list of workouts when their work was the fastest of the day.

"I think he could have gone a few laps at that pace, not just three-eighths of a mile," Ashleigh said with a laugh. "He went a little faster than I would have liked, but I didn't want to frustrate him by trying to hold him too much."

"March to Glory's workout was sharp," commented a

tall, balding man as he passed the Whitebrook group. "His was the fastest of the twenty workouts posted so far today."

Ashleigh and Mike exchanged grins.

"Who was that?" Cindy asked eagerly.

"One of the clockers," Mike said. "Looks like we're not Glory's only fans anymore."

"At least we've put to rest the speculation that Glory runs fast only at Churchill Downs," Ashleigh said, dismounting. "I think he can handle any track and any surface."

"I'll take him back to the barn and cool him out." Cindy reached for Glory's reins, patting the big gray's shoulder with her other hand.

Ashleigh frowned. Cindy looked around and saw Flightful's trainer, Joe Gallagher, approaching their group.

"He's fast," the other trainer commented, looking Glory over. "Very fast. I still wonder what your secret is."

"No secret," Ashleigh said with an impatient sigh.

The other trainer shrugged. "Well, it should be a good race on Saturday. Flightful will be ready to take you on. March to Glory hardly seems to need preparation, though. He gets a little help from his friends before he runs, I guess." Joe walked off.

Ashleigh stared after him.

"What's the matter?" Cindy asked.

"I really don't like the tone of his remarks," Ashleigh said.

"What do you mean?" Cindy was worried.

Ashleigh shrugged. "He almost seemed to be accusing Whitebrook of something unfair—or illegal."

Well, that isn't possible, Cindy thought. *So we don't have anything to worry about.* "Come on, Glory," she said. "Let's go cool you off. You deserve a delicious sponge bath, then a nice walk."

As she led Glory toward the shed row she heard Mike say, "Let's hope the heat breaks before Glory's race."

Cindy stopped and hugged Glory's glossy neck. "Heat or no heat, you'll win your race—I just know it!"

Cindy spent the afternoon watching the races with Samantha and Ashleigh. None of the Whitebrook horses were running, but Cindy knew that both young women liked to watch a few races every day at the meets. That way they could see how the track was playing and evaluate the competition for future races. Samantha had arrived at the track at lunchtime after a record-fast drive up from Kentucky. Cindy knew that her older sister had been anxious to see Shining.

Cindy jumped up in the stands as the horses roared into the stretch in the fourth race of the afternoon. *This may be work for Ashleigh and Samantha, but they've got a great job,* Cindy thought. *They like watching the races as much as I do!*

"Go, Sensational Time!" Ashleigh yelled, punching the air. "Reach for it!"

"Yes!" Samantha shouted as Sensational Time, a rangy bay colt, found another gear and zipped under the wire just in front of the favorite.

Before each race Ashleigh, Samantha, and Cindy went

down to the walking ring to look at the horses before they entered the track. Ashleigh gave Cindy and Samantha tips on handicapping. Cindy was amazed at how Ashleigh could look quickly at each horse and judge from its movements whether it was slightly sore or feeling off that day and wouldn't run its best. Then Ashleigh and Samantha pored over the *Daily Racing Form* and eliminated other horses from contention based on past track performances. They picked a lot of winners.

Cindy cheered with Samantha and Ashleigh through a full card of races. Cindy had quickly caught on to how to handicap. "Yes!" she said with satisfaction when the horse she had chosen won the last race of the day.

"Not bad, Cindy," Ashleigh said as they walked back to the Whitebrook shed row.

"That was fun." Cindy grinned.

"Boy, am I tired," Ashleigh said. "Maybe someday I'll be a sedate old lady and not get worked up about horse races."

"I doubt it." Samantha laughed. "I mean, we'll get old, but I think all three of us will still be screaming our heads off at races and waving our canes."

"You bet," Cindy said through a yawn. She wondered if she had time for a little nap in Glory's stall before dinner. She liked the idea. When she had first come to Whitebrook, she'd spent a cozy night in a stall with Rainbow and Four Leaf Clover. It would be fun to sleep in Glory's stall.

Suddenly Cindy spotted Max standing in front of one of the barns. "Hey, Max!" she called.

Max turned and waved.

"Is it okay if I meet you back at the barn in a little while?" Cindy asked Samantha.

"Sure. I think we're just going to grab something at the track kitchen for dinner," Samantha said. "Probably in about an hour."

"Would you tell Dad and Beth where I am?"

"Yeah. Have fun." Samantha smiled, and so did Ashleigh. *Oh, great, now Ashleigh thinks Max is my boyfriend,* Cindy thought. She ignored their grins and dashed over to Max, forgetting how tired she was. He was wearing a black T-shirt with a white racehorse on the front and NEW YORK CITY written on the back. His face was a dark tan.

"So when did you get here?" he asked.

"Yesterday." Cindy pushed back her hair. She realized she hadn't given much thought to her appearance since her family had gotten to the track. "Where's your mom?" she asked.

"She's visiting some of her patients. We just got here this morning."

"What are you going to do now? You sure don't need to work on your suntan," Cindy said.

Max smiled. "I've been *baking* in the sun on the rounds with my mom. In case you didn't notice when you went with us, we spend a lot of time out in the paddocks. And the trees are never in the right places."

"Yeah, I noticed." Cindy was glad to see Max. They could do a lot of things together.

"I was just about to check out the horses. You want to come?" he asked.

"Sure! I haven't had time to do that yet."

They set off between the shed rows. "Who do you want to see first?" Max asked.

"Hmmm." Cindy considered. There were dozens of quality racehorses at the Belmont summer meet. In a few weeks the Belmont Stakes would be run, and some of the famous horses who would race in it were already there. But Cindy was most interested in Glory's competition. "Let's go see Flightful," she said. "His work this morning was a little faster than Glory's and Flightful's trainer is making a big deal out of it, even though Ashleigh was holding Glory back."

"Maybe Flightful used himself up," Max said.

"That's kind of what I'm hoping." Cindy would never want a horse to be hurt, but she wouldn't mind if Flightful was a little tired after his morning exercise.

"Do you know which barn Flightful is in?" Max asked.

"Yeah," Cindy said. "It's right over there, almost next to ours. I asked my dad where it was this morning. He told me to stay out of Joe Gallagher's hair, though—that's Flightful's trainer. I don't think Joe likes Whitebrook much, since Glory beat his horse in their last matchup."

Cindy stood in front of the barn for a minute, trying to get up the nerve to go in. She wasn't even sure if they were allowed to. But there was only one way to find out.

"Come on," she said to Max. "Let's just act normal."

"My mom said Flightful's owners used a little-known dam and sire on purpose in breeding him," Max said as they walked along the aisle, looking in stalls. "They were trying to get a sounder horse that could go the distance."

"My dad always says if you breed quality to quality,

that's what you get," Cindy whispered. "Here's Flightful's stall—it's got his nameplate on it."

Flightful sniffed in their direction and pricked his ears. The black horse was no beauty, Cindy noted. He had a slightly Roman, or curved, nose and a thick neck. Flightful walked to the door of his stall to investigate his visitors. He seemed like a nice horse.

"All right, kids, get away from there."

Cindy turned and saw Joe Gallagher striding toward them.

"Okay," she said meekly. Maybe if she and Max slipped out quietly, Gallagher would just let them go.

"Find somewhere else to play," Joe said. He sounded nice, but Cindy didn't think he meant it.

"Sure," Max said, walking quickly down the aisle with Cindy. "We just wanted to see your horse. He's great."

"Okay—but bye now."

Cindy was glad to get out into the light and bustle of the stable yard again. She looked over her shoulder and saw that Joe was still watching them from the doorway. "I hope he doesn't tell my dad," she said, a trace of worry in her voice.

"I don't think he will," Max reassured her. "He thought we were just dumb kids."

"Well, at least I got a close look at Flightful before Joe kicked us out," Cindy said. "I don't think that horse can beat Glory."

"Glory's way out of Flightful's class," Max agreed.

"I'd better get back to Glory now," Cindy said. "We've got weeks to look at the other horses—we can do that another time."

"I'll come with you to see Glory," Max said.

At Whitebrook's shed row Len and Mike were sitting in front of Glory's stall, reading newspapers.

"Hi, you two," Mike said.

"Hi," Cindy said, looking in on Glory.

The colt was standing on three legs with his tail to the door. At the sound of her voice he swung around and whinnied joyously. "Are you ready for some attention?" she asked.

Glory walked to the door and leaned over, checking Cindy's pockets. "Yes, I've got a carrot for you," Cindy said. "You'd be so disappointed if I didn't."

Glory crunched the carrot with satisfaction. Then he looked at Max inquisitively. Glory had learned that Max was also usually good for a treat.

Max laughed and pulled a carrot out of his jeans pocket. "Just for you, Glory."

"He looks great, Cindy," Len said.

Mike flipped a page of his newspaper. "I don't see how Glory could be more ready for the race Saturday."

Cindy smiled and rubbed the colt's glossy neck. Even Mike didn't have any doubts about him. *I'm really looking forward to this race,* she thought with a happy sigh. *In fact, I can't wait.*

8

"WHAT A SCORCHER OF A DAY," IAN SAID ON SATURDAY, reaching for the soda beside his seat in the grandstand.

"It's muggy, too." Beth fanned her face with her program and laughed. "Well, that didn't do much good—I just moved the hot air around."

"Hmmm," Cindy said absently. Through binoculars she was watching Glory on the track. The horses had just begun to file out for the post parade of Glory's first stakes race.

Cindy frowned, adjusting the focus on the binoculars. Usually the post parade was one of her favorite events at the track. The high-spirited racehorses, eager to run, arched their necks and pranced as they walked or trotted along the track with their jockeys. That day the jockeys' silks were bright patches of color against the hazy, shrouded landscape.

But Cindy didn't like what she saw now. Glory was

sweating far more than usual. His neck was lathered white already, and dark patches showed at his flanks. Either Glory was reacting badly to the hot weather, or for some reason he was nervous.

Being nervous really does make you sweat, Cindy thought. Worrying about Glory was making her own palms damp.

"March to Glory sure is all sweated up," a man near Cindy said. "I wonder why. Flightful looks cool as a cucumber."

Cindy groaned inwardly. Flightful did look composed. The black colt was walking quietly along, showing perfect manners. But Glory wasn't acting up—he was just sweating, Cindy thought. Something might be wrong with him. Now she was really nervous.

Why wasn't I nervous about the race before? she asked herself. *I should have been.* She knew that so many factors went into a horse's winning a race, even if he was fast. European horses often did poorly on U.S. tracks because they couldn't stand the heat and humidity. Glory might have the same problem in the hot weather at Belmont.

Cindy remembered how stiff the competition was at this level of racing. Several of the horses in the field had already won a stakes race, including Northern Sights, a powerful-looking bay who was coming off a grade-two win at Hollywood Park, and Thatsa Dream, a blue roan who had won several races at Churchill Downs in the spring. This wasn't an easy race for Glory against maidens or claimers.

"Sammy, do you think Glory's okay?" Cindy asked.

Her older sister sat next to her, also gazing through binoculars.

"I don't know," Samantha said honestly, setting down the binoculars. "I've never seen him look like that."

"He was all right in the saddling paddock. I don't know what happened." Cindy drew a deep breath and watched the horses begin their warm-ups. Glory broke into a swift, graceful canter, his long black-and-gray mane and tail flowing like a river of silk. Ashleigh easily stayed with him, riding as if she were part of the horse. They were a beautiful pair.

Ashleigh let Glory out a little. The big horse responded instantly as if to say, *We're in this together.*

"This is just a sprint," Mike said, leaning around Ian to talk to Samantha and Cindy. "Ash is probably letting Glory work off a little tension. He should still have plenty of energy left."

"Ashleigh is such an incredible jockey," Samantha said.

"I know. I can't believe how lucky I am that she rides him." Cindy felt a rush of gratitude toward Ashleigh.

Cindy began to relax as Ashleigh guided Glory toward the starting gate. This was what she had always dreamed of for Glory, she reminded herself. He was running in a stakes race, among the best racehorses in the country.

"If Glory wins here at Belmont, people really will know that Glory's a great horse," Cindy said.

"That's true," Samantha agreed. "Nobody can say he wins just because the competition is second-rate allowance horses."

Cindy watched an attendant lead Glory into the gate.

As usual, he loaded like an angel. Glory had drawn the number-one slot, an excellent post position. He would be right along the inside rail, well positioned to go straight to the lead. Flightful was in the number-five slot in the field of nine.

Come on, Glory, Cindy willed her horse. *This is the big time. But I know you can win!*

The other horses were loaded quickly into the gate. For a moment there was silence, as if the hot, oppressive air were stilling all sound. Almost instantly the gate sprang open and the starting bell shrilled into the quiet.

Glory broke fast from the gate, charging into the lead.

"March to Glory has left the gate full of run," called the announcer. "He's been sent immediately to the lead. Flightful is a close second."

"I wonder if this will be a rematch of the last race," Mike shouted over the cheers of the crowd.

"No, it isn't!" Cindy cried, half rising from her seat. "Glory's pulling away!"

Glory was soaring, taking tremendous strides as he left the black horse behind in the dust. Cindy could almost feel Glory's pleasure in the quick, effortless touch of his feet on the ground before he was airborne again.

The horses roared around the turn. "And March to Glory is driving on the lead!" the announcer shouted.

Cindy saw that Flightful's jockey wasn't giving up easily. He went for his whip. The black horse increased his speed marginally.

"Felipe's asking Flightful for run, but he's not giving it," Ian said.

"Nobody's going to catch Glory today!" Cindy pounded her program on the seat back in front of her. She held her breath. Glory was five lengths in the lead and gaining with every fraction of a second.

"Doesn't look like it," Mike agreed.

Flightful's jockey swerved the black colt in toward the rail just as Thatsa Dream surged forward.

"No!" Cindy gasped. Even from this distance she could see that Felipe didn't have room to get Flightful in front of the other colt.

Flightful's hindquarters hit the bay horse's shoulder. Cindy saw Thatsa Dream's jockey frantically yank his mount's head to the outside just as Flightful charged by him. The black horse barely missed the rail and kept going.

"Thank goodness." Cindy sighed with relief.

"I'll bet the conversation between the two jockeys out there was hot and furious," Ian commented. "Look at Glory go!"

Glory was streaking for the wire. Head high, he was galloping merrily along, ten lengths ahead of the field. He was the only horse in his race again.

"Flightful is dropping out of contention!" Samantha said.

"He may have injured himself in that collision," Mike remarked.

Glory flashed under the wire, a streak of molten silver. "Yes, Glory!" Cindy screamed. She was already getting up to go to the winner's circle before the other horses had even crossed the finish. As she hurried down the steps she noticed that the board in the infield was lit up with the INQUIRY sign. That would be about Flightful's collision with Thatsa Dream—the bay colt's jockey would have lodged a protest. No one could doubt that Glory was the winner, though, she thought.

The horses were jogging toward the gap, their jockeys standing high in the stirrups. Exercise riders and trainers went quickly out to meet them.

"Well, Glory romps to victory again!" Ashleigh called as she rode up.

"You couldn't have been better, boy!" Cindy hugged Glory happily as Ashleigh dismounted. The colt heaved a big sigh, then rubbed his muzzle against her hair. He was dripping sweat all over, Cindy noticed with alarm. The race in the heat seemed to have taken a lot out of him. Glory was breathing in quick huffs.

Ashleigh's expression changed to one of concern as she examined Glory. "Cool him out carefully, Cindy," she said. "In this heat he really had to put out an effort. I'd walk him an extra half hour. Then rehydrate him slowly."

Cindy nodded, already reaching for Glory's lead shank.

"What happened with Flightful?" Mike asked Ashleigh, gesturing toward the board. "That was as clear a case of interference as I've ever seen."

"Flightful's jockey told me his orders were not to give up ground." Ashleigh shrugged. "I'm glad we didn't get in his way."

Ashleigh allowed just one quick picture of Glory in the winner's circle, then Cindy began to lead him toward the barn.

"We'll walk for at least an hour," Cindy told the colt, rubbing his forehead. "Then when you're completely cool, I'll give you a carrot. And once we get away from all these people and it isn't showing off, I'm going to tell you at least ten more times how great you did!"

Glory blew a gentle breath on her shoulder, as if he were relieved she was taking care of him. He seemed to be breathing more easily now, she noted with relief.

"Mike, Glory's won his first three starts going away," called a reporter. "In your opinion, is this horse the next Just Victory?"

Cindy kept walking, because Glory couldn't be left standing still until he was thoroughly cooled out; otherwise his muscles could tie up. But she had to restrain herself from squealing with joy at the reporter's words. She strained her ears to hear more.

"We'll see," Mike said. "Glory will definitely be racing again soon. No, we haven't decided when yet. But Just Victory set six track records and won thirteen of sixteen starts. I think it would be premature to conclude that Glory's the next Just Victory after just three wins and one track record."

Cindy closed her eyes in sheer bliss. *No, it wouldn't be. I knew it all along,* she thought. *So did Ben.*

"Go with Max and have fun," Samantha urged Cindy the next day.

Cindy hesitated and looked back at Glory's stall. She could barely see him, because a crowd of reporters had gathered in the barn. Ever since Glory's brilliant race the previous day the reporters had been trying to interview Ashleigh, Mike, Cindy's dad, or anyone else from Whitebrook who would talk to them.

Max had just stopped by the barn and invited Cindy to go sightseeing in New York that afternoon with him and his mother. Cindy wanted to go, but she wasn't sure if she should leave Glory. She never liked to leave him when he was at the track, because she was sure he preferred to have company when he was in a strange place. And she was still a little worried about him. Glory had calmed down—the case of nerves he'd had before the race or the effects of the heat seemed to have disappeared completely. But maybe she should watch him a little longer, Cindy thought.

"You don't need to stay with him," Ashleigh said. "He came out of the race just fine. He's taking today off, too."

"I don't know." Cindy frowned. "After the way he ran yesterday, he deserves a lot of attention."

Samantha laughed and pointed at Glory's stall. "Do you see all those reporters Len and Mike are trying to chase away from him? He's not going to be lonesome if you're gone for the afternoon."

Cindy looked at Glory. The gray colt was tossing his head and hanging it as far over his stall door as he could. Obviously he was just as interested in the visitors as they were in him. "Okay," she said. "I'll be back for dinner."

Dr. Smith and Max were waiting in front of one of the shed rows. "Great, you can come!" Max said.

"I checked over Glory," Dr. Smith said. "The way he reacted to the heat was perfectly normal. Don't worry about him, Cindy. Jim will be here to call me about any crises."

Cindy saw Jim standing just inside the barn. His gaze was cold, as usual. *Oh, well—he seems to know what he's doing,* she thought.

"Where do you want to go first?" Max asked as they walked to the Smiths' car.

"The Empire State Building." Cindy wanted to see the famous view of Manhattan from the top.

Dr. Smith drove skillfully through the city and parked near the Empire State Building. Cindy got out of the car and stood still for a second, trying to get her bearings. The people on the sidewalk were all moving so fast, it was dizzying. Not smacking into anyone there was much more complicated than riding on a crowded track at home, she thought.

Cindy closed her eyes as the elevator rocketed them to the top of the building. She liked speed—but not going straight up!

On the observation deck she and Max looked out over the vast city.

"This is some view," Max said.

"It sure is." Cindy couldn't believe how many people lived in Manhattan. She knew from her guidebook that, surprisingly, a lot of horses lived or worked in the city, too. Carriage horses took tourists around the city, a stable near Central Park rented horses to ride, and police horses patrolled the streets.

After the Empire State Building they went for burgers

and exotic chocolate desserts at a café with a rock-and-roll theme. Cindy bought two T-shirts with the café's name on them for Heather and Mandy, carefully selecting the right sizes. She hadn't heard from her friends in the week since she'd left Kentucky, and Cindy realized that she missed them. She wondered how Heather's jumping lessons were going and if Mandy had solved the problem with her blisters.

I should write Heather and Mandy tonight and tell them all the news about how Glory won and my afternoon in the city, Cindy thought. *Things just couldn't be going better.*

"I need to get back," Dr. Smith said, spooning up a last bite of dessert. "I've got some horses to look at tonight."

"I should check on Glory," Cindy agreed.

Back at Belmont, Cindy said good-bye to the Smiths in the parking lot and hurried toward the Whitebrook stabling. She was sure Glory was fine, as everyone had said, but she still needed to see for herself.

Suddenly Cindy saw Lavinia Townsend directly in front of her. There was no time to avoid her.

Cindy supposed she should have been prepared to see the Townsends. They came to New York every year to race their horses and, later in the summer, relax in their lavish country house at Saratoga.

"We all should have known," Lavinia said as she approached.

Cindy was confused. "Known what?"

Lavinia shook her head. "Why Whitebrook's horses are on a winning streak."

"I guess so," Cindy said. She didn't have the faintest idea what Lavinia was talking about. Lavinia was glaring at her, but there was something else in her expression. Cindy was sure Lavinia looked satisfied as she turned away.

"Something's happened," Cindy murmured, starting to run. "Please, please don't let it be to Glory."

In front of the Whitebrook shed row a huge crowd had gathered. It was much bigger than it had been when Cindy left. *What do they want now?* she thought. *I've never seen so many reporters and photographers, even after Shining's races. But no Whitebrook horses ran today.*

Not everyone looked like a reporter, she realized. Several people in suits seemed to be track officials. They were trying to clear away the press. Cindy saw Ashleigh at the center of the mob. Ashleigh's face was very pale. "No comment. No comment," she kept saying to the barrage of questions everyone was shouting at her.

Cindy's heart sank as she realized that the crowd was in front of Glory's stall.

"Cindy, could you come here?" Ashleigh called. "There's trouble with Glory."

Cindy fought her way through the crowd to Ashleigh. "What's wrong?" she asked fearfully.

"As the winner of his race, Glory was tested for illegal drugs." Ashleigh's voice was strained. "He tested positive and has been disqualified."

FEELING NUMB, CINDY FOLLOWED ASHLEIGH AWAY FROM THE shed row.

"Let's go somewhere we can talk," Ashleigh said. "This place is a zoo."

Cindy noticed the stares they were getting. Most of the looks were openly cold and hostile. She couldn't believe how quickly Glory had gone from being the wonder horse to being in total disgrace.

"Well, now we know how March to Glory ran so fast in his first two races," she heard an older man say.

"The trainer probably uses drugs, too," said his companion, a well-dressed young woman. "He'd have to, or he wouldn't think of trying something like this."

Cindy's face flushed in anger. She opened her mouth to tell the woman that her father had never touched drugs and would never give a horse a drug except to medicate it.

Ashleigh took Cindy's arm. "Come on," she said.

"Don't answer them now. We should consult with Mike and Ian and maybe get legal counsel before we talk to anyone."

The positive drug test is what Lavinia meant, Cindy realized. *No wonder she looked happy.* Cindy felt tears spring to her eyes as the full weight of what had happened hit her.

"I should be with Glory," she said, her voice cracking.

"He's all right, Cindy." Ashleigh unlocked the doors to her car in the parking lot. "Len is watching him, and we just paged Dr. Smith. She'll get there in a minute. The track vet already examined him."

"Is he sick from the drug?" Cindy asked miserably. "What was it?"

"Procaine. That's a common drug to test positive for. He's not showing any effects, at least not right now." Ashleigh frowned thoughtfully. "Probably he got a relatively small dose, like in a penicillin shot. Although now I'm wondering if he was so sweated up yesterday because of this, since procaine can act as a stimulant."

"I need to see him," Cindy said. "The crowd may be upsetting him." Glory wouldn't know what was happening, and he might be frightened.

"We'll go back in an hour—everyone will leave the barn area if there's no one to talk to."

Cindy was silent during the drive to the motel. She tried to think how Glory could have tested positive for a drug, but her mind refused to work.

Ashleigh picked up her car phone. "I'm going to call the barn and see if Dr. Smith has gotten there yet." In a few moments someone answered at the barn, and Ashleigh nodded to Cindy. "She's there. Glory's okay." Ashleigh spoke to the vet a few moments longer, then hung up the phone with a sigh.

"How did Glory get drugged?" Cindy asked.

"I don't know." Ashleigh's mouth was set in a grim line. "Right now I'm hoping that it *didn't* happen—the lab that tested the sample may have made a mistake. Of course I immediately asked for a retest by another lab."

Cindy sat up a little straighter. Maybe that was what this was—a simple mistake.

Ashleigh turned left into the motel parking lot. "The others are waiting in the restaurant," she said. "We definitely need to have a council of war about this." At Ashleigh's serious tone, Cindy's hopes sank again.

Ian, Beth, Mike, and Samantha were sitting at a table in the restaurant, drinking coffee. Cindy thought they looked as stunned as she felt.

"What's the latest word on Glory?" Ian asked as Cindy and Ashleigh sat down.

"He seems perfectly fine," Ashleigh said.

Cindy closed her eyes in relief. She couldn't hear those words too many times.

"Okay, let's get to the bottom of this," Mike said. "How did Glory get a dose of procaine? He hasn't been on penicillin for an infection or anything, has he?"

Ashleigh shook her head. "I spoke to Dr. Smith first thing about that. Glory's never been on any medication. He's remarkably healthy."

"Everyone is saying Glory was on drugs all along and that nobody found out until now," Cindy cried.

"That's not possible," Ashleigh said. Cindy could tell that Ashleigh was struggling to stay calm. "The winner of every race is tested for drugs, and the tests are highly sensitive. Glory tested negative in his first two races. So he definitely won them without drugs. Certainly without procaine." Ashleigh rubbed her forehead. "We'll figure this out," she said. "There has to be some explanation."

"I can't think what." Samantha shook her head.

"Well, since Glory wasn't supposed to have any drug, according to Dr. Smith, maybe someone drugged him so that exactly this would happen," Ashleigh said bluntly. "Maybe somebody wanted Glory to lose his race."

"I guess that could be true," Ian said wearily.

"Someone could have given Glory the procaine before we even left home," Ashleigh went on. "It has a very long clearance time."

"Maybe the vet had something to do with it," Mike said. "The most likely explanation is that she mixed Glory up with another horse that was supposed to get the procaine for medicinal reasons. Now she's afraid to admit it. Or she's in collusion with somebody and injected the procaine on purpose."

Cindy gasped in surprise. Mike couldn't really think Dr. Smith had done this. "Dr. Smith isn't dumb," Cindy defended her. "And she's not dishonest."

"No, I don't think so, either," Ashleigh agreed. "But those are logical explanations if you don't know Dr. Smith."

100

"Who would do such a horrible thing?" Cindy felt frantic. Someone was trying to hurt her beloved horse.

"I don't know." Ashleigh stared at the ceiling. "Possibly this is directed at Whitebrook."

"How come?" That didn't make any sense to Cindy. But Mike was nodding.

"The track got the results back on Glory so fast because they had a tip that he was drugged," he said. "Whitebrook's a pretty high-profile farm these days. We've had a lot of winners."

That was what Lavinia had said, Cindy remembered.

"I've got my share of enemies," Ian said wearily. "And the result of the positive drug test is that I'm suspended. I can't train until my suspension runs out or this is cleared up."

Samantha furrowed her forehead. "That's right."

"We're all under a cloud," Beth said. "I mean, everyone in the racing business knows we're a family operation."

"If this had happened at one of the California tracks, I might not be in nearly as much trouble," Ian said. "A trainer at one of them was recently given only a small fine and fifteen days suspension when his horse tested positive for desmethyl pyrilamine, an antihistamine that can act as a stimulant."

"I remember." Ashleigh nodded. "The stewards stayed the suspension because of the trainer's previous good record. But he's on probation for the rest of the year."

Ian signaled the waitress for more coffee and sighed. "Well, the racing officials in New York didn't cut me any slack," he said. "Except for furosemide, at Belmont a horse can't test positive even for an aspirin." Cindy knew that furosemide was a drug given to horses whose lungs would otherwise bleed when they ran.

"That's not really a bad rule," Ashleigh remarked.

"No," Ian said. "Under most circumstances I'd agree."

"But what's going to happen?" Cindy cried. It had just sunk in what this would mean for Glory. "You have to help us train Glory!"

"I can still give you advice, of course." Ian's voice was strained. "But I can't stand at the rail and officially train. I'm suspended for sixty days, pending appeal. I could reduce that to forty-five if I accept the penalty, but of course I'm not going to—I didn't do anything wrong. So I'll be out of commission for a while. I needed to work with Shining for the Suburban next month," Ian added grimly. "That's not going to happen now, either."

"I'll have to take over as trainer of both horses," Mike said.

Cindy stared at her father. She couldn't believe this was happening.

Ian gave her a small smile. "You and Mike and the others can bring Glory through."

"This is so unfair," Cindy muttered.

"Not really." Ian rubbed the back of his neck. "I'm Glory's trainer. That means I'm responsible for his welfare. Even though I didn't give him an illegal drug, I'm absolutely responsible for making sure no one else does. I let Glory down."

"No, you didn't," Cindy said quickly. Someone had let Glory down—but that person definitely wasn't her father.

102

*   *   *

That evening Ian and Ashleigh drove Cindy back to the track to see Glory. "I want to check on him, too," Ashleigh said to Cindy as they walked to the shed row. "We looked at him closely this afternoon before you got here, but I don't think we can be too careful."

"I shouldn't have left him," Cindy said miserably. She could never forgive herself for that. She'd gone off and enjoyed herself in New York while Glory was drugged.

"Cindy, your being here wouldn't have changed anything," Ian said, squeezing her shoulder. "Glory could have gotten the procaine anytime during the past two weeks. You can't be on twenty-four-hour guard with him."

"Sounds like a good idea," Cindy murmured. She certainly wasn't going to leave the colt alone one minute more than she had to now.

Len was sitting on a chair in front of Glory's stall, listening to the news on the radio.

"All quiet here," he said. "Finally everybody decided to leave us alone."

"How's Glory?" Cindy asked, running to the stall. He wasn't looking out over the door the way he usually did. She was terrified at the thought of what she might see. What if Glory was drenched with sweat again or down on the ground, writhing in pain? Nothing could be done to get the drug out of his system faster—it would just have to clear gradually.

Suddenly Glory poked his head over the stall door and

looked over Len's shoulder. He seemed to be trying to read the newspaper.

Cindy started to laugh but choked on tears. "Glory, you're so funny," she said.

At the sound of her voice Glory's ears pricked and he whickered throatily. Cindy walked over to him and took his head in her arms. In the muted barn light his gray coat gleamed softly, like fine pewter. He looked perfectly healthy. "What happened to you, boy?" she whispered. "Who did this to you?"

"I really don't know who would do something like this, or why," Ian said.

"That's one of the good things about horses," Len said. "They just want to run. They don't understand the politics involved."

A lump formed in Cindy's throat. Glory was affectionately rubbing his muzzle against her shirt. He didn't understand that something was wrong with him or that because of his positive drug test, Whitebrook's reputation was tarnished.

"Is he really okay, Len?" she asked.

"Dr. Smith's been to see him twice, and she said the concentration of the drug in his blood isn't high enough anymore to bother him," Len reassured her. "He almost certainly won't suffer any ill effects from it, either."

"The sabotage does seem to be directed at Whitebrook rather than the horse." Ashleigh frowned.

"I'll be on my guard tonight," Len promised.

"Well, if nothing else happens, this doesn't have to be a major setback for Glory," Ashleigh said with a sigh. "In a few days we'll run him in front of the track veterinarians, and then he'll be tested again for drugs. If he's clean, he could race soon."

"There are worse drugs he could have been given—worse for him and for me," Ian said. "I guess we should be grateful. If he'd been given a narcotic like fentanyl or morphine, he might show dramatic effects from it. And I'd be suspended for even longer."

Poor Dad is already suspended all summer, Cindy thought. She wondered if Glory's next drug test would really be the end of the matter. Glory whickered to her lovingly, but he couldn't tell her, either.

"Shining looks perfect," Samantha said the next afternoon. The horses had just come out onto the track for the grade-one Metropolitan Handicap. Shining was tossing her head and prancing. Her finely toned muscles bunched and released, and her red-and-white coat sparkled in the filtered sunshine. The heat still hadn't broken.

Cindy noticed that Samantha's voice was tense, much more so than usual when Shining ran. Cindy knew why. Shining was getting a lot of publicity, but not the kind anyone from Whitebrook wanted. The talk on the backside, in the grandstand, and even in the parking lot was about whether not just Glory but all the Whitebrook horses ran on illegal drugs.

"You'd better believe they're going to test Shining almost to death after the race for every possible drug—whether she wins or not," Samantha said grimly.

The crowd was booing. Cindy sat up straighter in shock. They were booing Ashleigh!

Cindy saw that Ashleigh was trying to be professional about it. She kept Shining going at a steady canter clockwise around the track.

"Shining should run a good race," Beth said, taking Samantha's hand. "She's going in as the favorite."

Samantha nodded, but Cindy saw tears in her eyes. "Shining's not going to walk away with it, though," Samantha said. "The race is a mile long. Shining has run outstandingly at over a mile, but Deputation and First Sea both won their last races decisively at a mile flat. Ashleigh will have to make sure Shining doesn't get caught at the wire."

Shining skittered sideways. Ashleigh straightened her out, but the roan mare continued to yank on the reins. She almost bumped Deputation, whose jockey was cantering by on the outside. Deputation's jockey had to pull the dark gray horse up short.

Cindy groaned. Shining usually behaved perfectly. Cindy wondered if Ashleigh had been upset by the crowd and it was affecting her riding. Cindy only hoped Ashleigh could get the mare focused by post time.

The horses were loaded into the gate. Cindy noted grimly that five horses, or half the field, balked going in.

"I'll bet the continued heat is making all the horses cranky," Beth remarked.

"I don't think Shining has ever run in heat this intense," Ian agreed.

At last the number-ten horse was in. Cindy held her breath, waiting for the starting bell.

Shining reared in the gate! Ashleigh almost fell off over Shining's side. At the last second Ashleigh hung on, her hands buried in Shining's mane.

Cindy gasped. "Shining never did that before!" she cried.

"No. I hope she's not coming apart," Mike said tersely. The color had drained from his face. Cindy knew how close Ashleigh had come to falling off—and possibly getting trampled by the excited horse's hooves.

Track attendants climbed up on the adjoining gate slots and grasped Shining's bridle to steady her. Ashleigh righted herself—and the next second the gate flew open.

"Ashleigh's still not balanced in the saddle!" Mike cried.

The horses lunged out, but Shining hit the gate! Cindy watched in horror, a hand to her mouth. Could Ashleigh stay on? She was already half out of the saddle!

Shining seemed stunned for a moment. Then she gathered her legs beneath her and raced on. Her heart in her throat, Cindy watched as Ashleigh righted herself in a second. Shining dug in and roared after the other horses. Ashleigh positioned her along the rail, saving ground.

"They're doing it!" Cindy cried. "Oh, thank goodness!"

"Ashleigh seems to have her settled now." Ian sounded relieved.

"But they're seventh!" Samantha groaned, rubbing her forehead.

"Only nine lengths off the leaders," Mike said. "Don't

forget it's a mile race—Ashleigh's got time to catch the field."

The horses thundered around the far turn. Cindy glanced at the board and saw that Read by Me, the horse on the lead, was setting very fast fractions. She didn't see how the colt could maintain that pace for a mile. Cindy turned to her dad, a question on her lips. But as she watched, Read by Me began to drop back.

"Now Ashleigh's making her move!" Samantha gripped the edge of her seat in excitement.

Ashleigh had taken Shining to the outside of the first horse ahead of them. Ashleigh was crouched low over Shining's neck, asking for speed. The mare flattened out in response.

"And they're coming to the top of the stretch!" the announcer called.

Ashleigh and Shining were still in fifth. In front of them was a solid wall of four horses.

"Shining doesn't have anywhere to go!" Cindy clenched her jaw.

"Maybe something will open up," Beth said hopefully.

Cindy could see almost immediately that nothing would. The horses pounded past the quarter pole. Ashleigh was running out of time.

Suddenly Ashleigh moved Shining to the outside again. The mare was four wide and rolling. The horses in the wall ahead of Shining began to straggle out, and Shining gained on the number-two horse. Then she was in second place and bearing down on First Sea, the black horse on the lead!

"Come on, Shining!" Cindy screamed. "Please, girl!"

"She's out of ground!" Mike yelled. The two horses flashed under the wire with Shining behind by a neck.

"Darn!" Samantha cried.

"Shining really tried her best, though," Cindy said. She felt almost sick with disappointment.

"I know." Samantha gave her a strained smile.

Cindy sighed heavily. The race had been so difficult for Ashleigh. Shining hadn't seemed like herself, either.

"The crowd's booing Ashleigh again!" Mike said angrily as Ashleigh trotted Shining toward the gap. "How dare they—we ran an honest race!"

"Let's get down there," Ian said quietly, rising from his seat. "We don't want to leave Ashleigh to face them alone."

This is so awful, Cindy thought as they hurried out of the stands. *Ashleigh used to be the most popular jockey on the track.*

Ashleigh looked as close to tears as Cindy had ever seen her. Her blue-and-white silks and her face were covered with dust. Shining was breathing hard, her nostrils flared and showing red. Sweat dripped from her flanks and neck.

"Half the jockeys out there were on my case about our drug problem," Ashleigh said tiredly.

Shining hung her head and looked at Cindy. She seemed as unhappy as her jockey.

"Come on, Shining girl," Cindy said quickly. "Let's get you cooled out."

"Thanks." Ashleigh managed a crooked smile at Cindy. "She did her best. Give her the VIP treatment."

"I'll come with you," Samantha said to Cindy. "Good job, Ashleigh. This wasn't your fault—we can't win them all."

"Those jockeys are fine ones to talk about race fixing," Mike said angrily. "Gonzalez's job out there was to push the pace with Read by Me until most of the field tired. Then Schmidt mopped up with First Sea. Both horses are owned by the same stable."

"Well, even so, Shining never really fired." Ashleigh sighed. "I'm not sure I did, either. I'm not at all satisfied with my ride."

Cindy's heart went out to Ashleigh. The young jockey looked so discouraged. *We all feel terrible,* Cindy thought. *Who could be doing this to us?*

10

THAT EVENING CINDY LAY IN THE MOTEL ROOM, LISTLESSLY flipping through the TV channels. She had nothing else to do. No matter how much she had begged, pleaded, and threatened, her parents refused to let her sleep in Glory's stall.

She could still hear their voices in her head: *Len is perfectly capable of keeping watch over Glory. Nothing else is going to happen to him. You won't get any sleep in a stall.*

"I may not get any sleep if I stay with Glory, but I'm not going to get any sleep here, either," Cindy muttered. She couldn't stop thinking about what had happened and worrying about the colt. What if Glory's racing career was over? What if they couldn't figure out how he'd gotten the drug?

Cindy impatiently kicked off the covers. She belonged with Glory right now. Maybe she could make a difference. After all, whoever had drugged Glory had managed to get

111

to him the last time, despite Len's and everyone else's best efforts.

A knock sounded at the door. Cindy hesitated. She really didn't feel much like talking to anyone in her family after their argument.

"Cindy, it's me," Beth called. "I brought you something."

"Come in," Cindy said at last. It was lonesome in the room by herself, with nothing to do.

Beth opened the door and walked over to the bed. She was carrying a tray. "I brought you a fruit salad and milk from the restaurant. You didn't eat a thing for dinner."

"I'm not very hungry." Cindy pressed the button on the remote, changing the TV channel again. She didn't look at Beth. Cindy knew she was being a brat, but she couldn't help it.

"I know this is very hard," Beth said sympathetically, setting the bowl of fruit salad on the night table next to Cindy.

"It's worse than that." Cindy swallowed. "Whoever is poisoning Glory may kill him the next time."

"This could have been just an accident."

"Not with procaine." Cindy finally looked at Beth. "I talked to Dr. Smith about it. Glory could have gotten a drug like morphine or cocaine accidentally if a stable hand was using it and somehow contaminated his feed. But procaine is injected."

Beth sighed. "It's so hard to imagine that anyone would want to hurt Glory," she said quietly. "Everyone in the stable is on the alert now."

"I know." *But if I were in the stable with him, I wouldn't sleep,* Cindy thought. *I'd make completely sure he was safe.*

Beth rose. "I'll leave you alone. Sammy will be here in a little while."

"Where is she?" Cindy stared straight ahead, pretending to watch the music video on the screen.

Beth looked unhappy. "With Shining—trying to make sure for the thousandth time that she isn't drugged. Samantha's afraid that's why Shining lost the race today."

Cindy groaned. She had tried to tell herself that Shining couldn't possibly be drugged, too, and that Ashleigh had just ridden a bad race for once. *But if Sammy thinks Shining was drugged, I might have been unfair to Ashleigh,* she realized.

"Well, is Shining drugged?" Cindy asked, fear in her voice. She loved Shining. The red roan mare had been the first horse Cindy had groomed when she came to Whitebrook a year earlier. Shining was also the first Thoroughbred that Cindy had ever ridden.

"Sammy's not sure." Beth hesitated in the doorway. "Shining seems very tired. The official track results of the drug testing will be back in the morning, and Mike sent a sample to an independent lab."

"Oh, no!" Cindy wondered what they could expect to hear. Another procaine positive? This was all so crazy.

"Don't think the worst yet," Beth said. "We don't know that anything's wrong with Shining."

"Okay." Cindy closed her eyes. *Please let Mom be right,* she prayed.

"Try to eat a little," Beth said. "We may have some difficult days ahead of us. You need to keep up your strength."

Beth left the room, and Cindy looked at the luscious fruit salad on the table. She picked up a spoon and fished out a strawberry. *I'll bet Shining is drugged,* she said to herself. *That's the only explanation that makes sense for the way she ran today. What will happen to Glory next? Are you all right now, boy? Or are you in more danger?*

It was no use trying to eat. Cindy put down the spoon and picked up the remote. But she couldn't keep her mind on the TV.

"Hi," Samantha said, closing the motel room door behind her.

"What time is it?" Cindy rubbed her eyes.

"Almost one. Were you asleep?" Samantha sat down on the bed across from her and pulled off her boots.

"Not really." Cindy had managed to doze for a few minutes at a time, but almost instantly she found herself sitting bolt upright, panicking that someone was hurting Glory.

"Well, I can certainly sympathize." Samantha tossed her boots in a corner and looked at Cindy for a moment.

"How's Shining?" Cindy was almost afraid to ask.

"She seems all right." Samantha frowned. "The problem is, she didn't come out of the race very well. So it's hard for me to tell if she's drugged or just tired. She seems to be just tired. But that's not good, either."

"Why?"

"Because I'd planned to run Shining in the Suburban

114

Handicap in just a month," Samantha said. "For financial reasons it's important that she keep running in the biggest races—and winning them."

"I didn't realize Whitebrook needed the money," Cindy said slowly.

"Of course, we're not going to run Shining if there's any doubt about her fitness," Samantha said. "But if she can't run, Whitebrook is going to be in pretty serious financial trouble."

"Sagebrush and Matchless are running day after tomorrow," Cindy reminded her.

"Yes, but those are only allowance races. Even if they win, the purses won't amount to much. We had big hopes for Shining this summer, and Glory, too."

"I still have big hopes for Glory," Cindy said firmly. But she couldn't suppress a flicker of fear. She hadn't known the farm was badly in need of money. The situation was even worse than she had thought.

"I hope you're right in having them." Samantha flopped back on the pillows. "If the positive drug test was just a one-time thing, Glory will be out of the doghouse in a couple of days, after he runs before the track vets."

Cindy knew that after Dr. Smith had given Glory a clean bill of health, Mike had immediately set up a test for him with the track veterinarians. If Glory ran well before them and tested negative in another drug test afterward, he could race again. "I know he'll pass," she said. "He looks great, right?"

"He does," Samantha confirmed. "And maybe Shining

will recover in time for the Suburban. If not, I'll point her toward the Whitney in Saratoga."

"That's a big race," Cindy said hopefully. The winner would get a rich purse.

"Yeah. If Shining can't make the Suburban, that's horse racing, I guess." Samantha got up and began to putter around the bathroom, getting ready for bed.

Cindy felt a little better. Her older sister seemed to think that these ups and downs were part of the racing business and that everything was going to be all right in the end. For a minute Cindy had worried they might lose the farm. That had happened to Ashleigh years before, when a deadly virus had devastated her family's farm, Edgardale. The Griffens had been forced to sell the farm and all their surviving horses. It had taken a long time for Ashleigh to get over the pain of that loss.

"Oh, this came for you," Samantha said, returning to the bedroom. She tossed a letter to Cindy.

Cindy caught it and turned it over. The back of the envelope was stamped with a horse jumping. But even before she saw the stamp, Cindy recognized the bold, round handwriting. "It's from Mandy," she said.

"I got a letter from Tor today, too." Samantha smiled. "I wonder if they wrote them at the stable."

"Maybe. Mandy's probably spending a lot of time there." Cindy tore open the envelope. It was good to hear from somebody at home. This was the first letter she had gotten since she'd left for the track. Heather had already warned Cindy that she wasn't much of a letter writer.

I'm doing great, Mandy had written.

116

Cindy was surprised that the letter opened on such a positive note. When she had last seen Mandy, the little girl had been in agony from her jumping lessons.

I wonder if "great" to Mandy and Tor means her legs are one big blister from jumping ten hours a day! Cindy thought. She quickly read on.

My lessons are going perfectly, Cindy. Tor was right that I have to work hard or I'll never make the Olympics. But I had to do something about those blisters. So I asked my doctor what to do. I didn't ask him before, because I thought he might tell me to stop riding! But he didn't. I guess he knew it would be no use. He helped me put extra padding in my braces. I tried doing that before by myself, but the padding fell out. Now it doesn't, and I can really ride again!

Cindy could almost see Mandy on Butterball. Utterly fearless, Mandy was pointing the gallant little pony at challenging jumps and flying over them with room to spare. Cindy smiled for what felt like the first time in days. She admired her friend so much.

I can't give up, either, Cindy thought, folding the letter.

"Let's get some sleep." Samantha flicked off Cindy's music videos on the TV. "Otherwise we're all going to look like owls, with big circles under our eyes."

"Okay." Cindy got up to brush her teeth. *Then I'm going to sleep, whether I want to or not,* she thought determinedly. *Mandy got to the bottom of her problems. And so will I.*

11

"Hi," Max said, walking up to Cindy and Glory two days later. "What's new?"

"Not much." Cindy quickly stroked Glory's satiny coat with a dandy brush. She knew Max meant what was new about Whitebrook's drug problem. "I'm getting Glory ready to run before the track vets in an hour, so that they can check him out."

Glory tossed his head a little in the crossties, as if to emphasize her words.

"I know," Max said. "My mom and Jim will be there."

"Ashleigh, Mike, and my dad are hoping Glory will pass the test and that will be the end of it," Cindy said. "We still don't know who drugged Glory. But maybe it was just some kind of weird accident."

Glory craned his neck around to look at Max. He seemed to be asking Max's opinion.

"I think you'll do okay, boy," Max said encouragingly.

He got a brush out of Glory's tack trunk and began grooming his other side.

"I hope all of us do okay," Cindy said. "Even if Glory is clean now, everyone is still going to think Whitebrook runs horses on drugs. People stare at all of us and whisper. At least Shining tested negative after her race. Samantha was so happy, she almost cried."

"You still don't have any idea who did this?" Max asked, stroking Glory's neck. The gray horse leaned closer to Max and sighed, enjoying the caress.

"No." Cindy sighed, too, and removed a finishing cloth from Glory's tack trunk. She'd thought about the mystery almost nonstop, but she wasn't any closer to solving it.

Glory suddenly jerked away from Max. He shifted uneasily in the crossties and rolled his eyes back to look at Cindy.

"Easy, boy." Cindy stood very still for a moment, reminding herself to get a grip. She was nervous about how Glory would do in front of the track vets, and her nervousness seemed to be affecting him. The work for the vets was so important. Glory's whole racing career depended on it.

"If Glory passes, what race will he run in next?" Max asked.

"I don't know." Cindy ran the cloth over Glory's smooth flanks. The colt shivered with pleasure and stamped his foot, as if ordering her to continue. "I guess if he does all right today, Mike will pick another stakes race for him to run in soon." Nobody wanted to plan too far ahead for Glory until they were sure he was healthy, Cindy thought grimly.

Glory was pawing the concrete aisle. "Stop it, Glory!" she said. He was going to mess up his shoes, which had to be exactly right for him to run. She got the feeling they were making each other nervous now.

"What's the matter?" Max asked.

"Oh, nothing. I guess he's picking up on my mood." Cindy gave the colt a reassuring pat. Glory stopped pawing, but then he shivered, shaking his black-and-gray mane and tail. "I just don't think the drugging was an accident," Cindy said, rubbing Glory's shoulder vigorously to try to distract him from whatever was bothering him. "I mean, since procaine is used with penicillin and that's a common medicine, it does seem possible Glory got a shot meant for another horse or something like that. But I don't believe it."

"How come?" Max frowned.

"I thought about this most of the last two nights, when I couldn't sleep," Cindy said with a grimace. "Glory's former trainer, Ben Cavell, and some of the sportscasters have compared Glory to Just Victory. If Glory is the next Just Victory or an even greater racehorse, that would make a lot of people happy. I heard my dad say that then racing would have a new superstar, and attendance at the races and the TV audience would increase."

"So why would anyone want to drug Glory?" Max sounded puzzled.

"Because he's *too* good. Some people and horses are losing to him, like Joe Gallagher, Flightful's trainer.

120

Ashleigh said that Whitebrook might be the target of all this, because the farm was doing so well. But I think somebody just wanted to get Glory."

Max frowned. "So you think they might try to drug him again."

Cindy swallowed hard and nodded.

"He looks fantastic now," Max said. "I think this work will be a piece of cake."

"Thanks." Cindy looked Glory over. He did look perfect, she thought. With every movement his bulging muscles rippled under his taut, smooth dappled coat. His eyes were bright and his ears pricked, as if he couldn't wait to get on the track.

Glory was still tossing his head a little. Cindy frowned. The colt's neck had begun to sweat lightly. But the heat wave that had blanketed the track since they got there was still fierce, and the day was very warm.

"Ready to take him down?" Len asked, walking down the aisle. The old stable manager smiled reassuringly at Cindy.

Cindy nodded and reached to unclip Glory from the crossties. Glory stepped lightly sideways and shook his head again.

Suddenly he reared, his hooves slashing the air. It happened so fast, Cindy had no time to get out of the way. She felt the quick rush of wind as Glory's hooves missed her head by a fraction of an inch.

"Glory, get down!" she cried.

The crossties yanked hard on Glory's head. That seemed to upset him even more. With a squeal of rage he fought the ropes, twisting his head, pounding the wall with his front hooves. Cindy bit back a scream as he reared again, this time going so high he almost fell over backward.

Before she could think what to do, Len was at the colt's side. "Down, big guy," he said firmly, quickly attaching a lead line to Glory's halter and unfastening the crossties. "There's no need for this. Quiet down."

Shuddering, Glory stayed on all four feet. But the whites still showed in his rolling eyes.

"It's all right, boy," Cindy said, her voice trembling. "Please don't do that. Everything's going to be okay."

Suddenly Glory seemed to be himself again. He shook his head and shoved Cindy urgently with his nose, as if asking, *What happened to me?*

"You're fine now," Cindy said, smoothing his mane. She prayed that was true. She and Len exchanged worried glances.

"We'd better take him out there," Len said. "Otherwise folks will think the worst."

"I know." Glory stood quietly now. His sides were heaving, but he seemed to have settled down.

"Do you want to lead him?" Len asked. "He usually goes best for you."

Cindy nodded. "Come on, Glory," she said. "No more acting up. You've got to do your best." Cindy willed herself not to be afraid of the colt. She never had been before, but Glory wasn't acting like himself at all. She wasn't sure she could handle him if he reared like that again.

Glory nudged her hand hard. Cindy studied him for a second, from his elegant head down the proud arch of his neck to the sweep of his thick, long tail. She took a deep breath. No matter what happened, he was her horse and she loved him.

"Okay, Glory," she said. "Let's show them." She took the lead line from Len and walked the colt out of the barn. Glory followed her obediently.

"I'm going to stay back," Max called. "Glory doesn't know me as well as he knows you."

"I hope the fireworks are over." Cindy kept checking Glory as they walked toward the oval. He was skittering around a little, but not much more than usual. What she didn't like was the sweat darkening his neck and flanks. The sun, a red ball flanked by misty pink clouds, was blazing hot. Cindy pushed her damp bangs off her forehead. Maybe Glory was just reacting normally to the muggy weather.

At the track Ashleigh stood by the rail. Nearby were several track officials, talking among themselves. Len smoothed Glory's saddlecloth on his back and quickly saddled him up. Len's face was somber. Ashleigh walked slowly over.

"Hi, Glory boy," she said.

"Are you all right?" Cindy asked with concern. Ashleigh was very pale.

"I'm fine." Ashleigh managed a crooked smile. "I guess all the excitement is getting to me."

That's funny, Cindy said to herself. Ashleigh had ridden horses to victory in the Breeders' Cup, beating out the most seasoned jockeys and the greatest horses in the world. Cindy had seen the video, and Ashleigh had been the picture of composure. *But maybe this attack on Whitebrook's reputation is the toughest thing for her,* Cindy thought.

Ashleigh mounted up and gathered the reins. "Don't worry," she said. But Cindy saw her frown as she put Glory into a trot.

Cindy and Max joined Mike and Ian at the rail. "This is it," Ian said. His smile was tense. Cindy knew that his future as a trainer might be riding on the work. Dr. Smith and Jim were talking with the officials while they watched Glory.

Cindy looked quickly out to the track and her heart sank. "Oh, no," she murmured.

"What?" Max whispered.

"Look at how he's going." Cindy groaned softly. Glory's strides were choppy and uneven, and he was wildly tossing his head. Ashleigh had him under a tight hold. "He's trying to run away with her." Cindy balled her hands into fists. *Settle down, boy,* she willed the colt. *Now you've shown the officials how spirited you are. Just put in a good work.*

Suddenly Glory exploded. All four legs left the ground as he jumped almost straight in the air. He galloped madly up the track. Ashleigh had obviously been anticipating this, and Glory got away from her for only a few ragged strides before she pulled him around into a tight circle. Glory fought the restraint furiously, yanking on the reins and sidestepping. White lather flecked his sweat-soaked gray coat.

124

Out of the corner of her eye Cindy saw that the track vets were looking at Glory and frowning. Her heart gave a sickening lurch. *I don't like what I see, either,* she thought. *Glory, just stop it! I wish I could ride you.*

"Hold it!" Dr. Smith called out to Ashleigh. "I'm sorry," she said, turning to Mike and Ian. "I'm going to have to stop the work. Obviously something's wrong with this horse."

No! Cindy bit back a cry. *Glory can't be drugged again.* But looking at him, she knew it was true.

Cindy swallowed back tears. Ashleigh was turning Glory, trying to get him back to the gap. Even from this distance Cindy could see that Ashleigh wasn't having an easy time of it. Glory was half rearing, bouncing on his forelegs and shaking his head as he tried to yank the reins through her hands. Ashleigh looked exhausted. Glory whinnied urgently, as if he didn't want to act this way and was pleading for help.

Cindy ran out onto the track. Glory might be dangerous in his present state, but she had to help him— and Ashleigh.

Glory hardly seemed to know who she was. The big horse's frightened eyes rolled, and he let out another whinny of distress.

"Be careful, Cindy," Ashleigh said through gritted teeth. "He may go up again. I don't know what he'll do."

"I'll watch him." Haltingly they guided Glory to the gap. Cindy kept every muscle tense, ready to grab the colt, jump out of the way if he reared again, or whatever else it took just to keep him walking in a straight line. *This can't be happening,* Cindy thought, blinking furiously to keep her tears from blinding her. *I'll wake up and this will be just a nightmare.*

The track veterinarians were shaking their heads as Glory approached. Cindy knew what that meant.

"I'm going to have Glory tested right now," Dr. Smith said slowly. "It's pretty obvious he'll come up positive again."

The big gray colt reared, whinnying shrilly. His front hooves clawed the sky. "Glory, no!" Cindy cried. She pulled hard on the lead rope, trying to bring him down, but she was afraid the restraint would just upset him more. "Glory! Steady, boy." Cindy's voice shook. Glory seemed like a total stranger.

Len and Cindy had just brought the colt back from the testing barn. It would take a few hours to get the results, but everyone knew they would be positive. Nobody knew yet what drug they would find.

Len clipped a lead to the other side of Glory's halter. "Let's try walking him for a while," he said. "I can't see putting him back in the stall like this—he might hurt himself."

"Okay." Cindy hadn't stopped watching Glory for a second. The big horse's eyes were wild and glazed, and he was trembling. He whinnied again desperately.

"Let's go." Len and Cindy began walking Glory around the stable yard. Cindy saw to her misery that they had attracted another crowd. Glory half reared again, grunting in distress.

"Hush, sweetie! Glory, calm down!" Cindy tried not to panic. Glory scarcely seemed to hear her. What if the drug changed his whole personality and he would always be like this?

Dr. Smith and Jim walked up. "Does he seem any better to you?" Dr. Smith asked Cindy.

"Not really." Cindy braced herself as Glory backed up, shaking his head. "Easy, boy, easy." Cindy was terrified Glory would get away from her and run into the crowd. The gray horse snorted and lunged forward, burning the lead rope through Cindy's hands. Cindy barely managed to hang on to him.

"What can I do for him?" she asked, trying to keep the fear out of her voice.

"Not much, really—just what you're doing." Dr. Smith frowned. "If he gets any worse, I'll give him a tranquilizer. But let's see if the drug works its way out of his system without that. I don't want to fill him with more drugs, trying to counteract the effects of the first one."

Cindy shook her head. That didn't sound like a good idea to her, either. Glory stood frozen, his eyes still glazed, looking as if he were in another world.

"The track is rushing the sample out to the lab to be analyzed," Dr. Smith added. "They want to get to the bottom of this as much as we do. Drug scandals aren't good for racing's image."

"Or Whitebrook's," Len said grimly. "Let me help you with him, Cindy."

"No—it just makes him wilder when more people are around. I've got him." Cindy hoped that was true. Her arms already ached, and Glory was acting worse by the minute.

For the next several hours she tried to calm Glory down. Len watched from the doorway of the barn in case she needed help, but Cindy knew there wasn't much he could do. When Glory threw his worst fits, Cindy couldn't hold him back. She tried to stay clear of his hooves and waited them out. She was thankful that Dr. Smith had called the track guards, who had succeeded in getting rid of the press and other gawkers. Even Max had left—every time Glory saw his former friend approach, he had another attack of nerves.

Glory shot up again, squealing with rage and pain. Cindy let out the rope as much as she could while still keeping a loose hold on him. "Settle down, Glory," she pleaded quietly. "Don't fight it. Just try to relax."

Glory came down on all fours again and fretted, prancing in place and shaking his head. Flecks of white foam from his neck scattered in the dust. Cindy could do very little for him except keep him moving to distract him. She was terrified that if he kept rearing so high, he would fall over backward. She ground her teeth in frustration.

Finally Glory stood still. He dropped his head almost to the ground. Then he looked up at Cindy and snorted softly. It was almost a question.

"Yes, boy," Cindy whispered. "I'm here." She walked toward him cautiously. Her arms felt like rubber from the strain, and her knees were buckling with exhaustion. As she approached him she staggered and almost fell.

Glory watched her come over. The craziness was gone

from his dark eyes, and he whickered throatily. "It's okay now, isn't it?" Cindy asked. She hugged him, pressing his sweat-soaked head against her wet shirt. The air smelled faintly salty, either from the nearby ocean or from her and Glory's sweat.

Cindy sank down on the ground and closed her eyes with relief. *I've never been so tired in my life,* she thought. But it was all right. She felt so peaceful.

Glory dropped his nose in her hair and gently whuffed. Cindy reached up a damp hand to touch the colt's wet, lathered neck. "We beat that drug, Glory," she murmured. "What was it this time?"

"Morphine. Glory tested positive for morphine," Dr. Smith announced later that afternoon.

Cindy looked over the half door of Glory's stall. The whole Whitebrook group was sitting on chairs outside the stall. They had been waiting for Dr. Smith to arrive and give them the test results.

Glory nudged Cindy aside and looked out, too. Cindy had sponged him off, dried him, and combed his mane and tail. He looked fine now, as if nothing had happened. He also had his usual curiosity back.

Cindy registered the horror on the faces of Ashleigh, Mike, Ian, and everyone else at Dr. Smith's words. She felt a sick lurch in her stomach. This was terrible news, and not just because Glory had been drugged again. Morphine was much worse than procaine. "Will he be okay?" Cindy asked, her voice trembling.

"Yes, I think so," Dr. Smith said. "But—"

"Somebody could have given Glory heroin," Max said. He sounded shocked. "You said horses metabolize it to morphine, right, Mom?"

"That's right." Dr. Smith blew out a breath and sat in a vacant chair.

"I know I sound like a broken record, but how could this have happened?" Mike ran a hand through his blond hair. "First procaine, now heroin?"

"Recently a horse tested positive for morphine at one of the California tracks," Dr. Smith said. "The horse had just won a stakes race. The trainer's barn was searched and evidence found of heroin abuse by a groom and a veterinary assistant. As Max said, horses can test positive for morphine after ingesting heroin. The groom and assistant were both suspended."

"To say nothing of what happened to the trainer." Ian's face was pale.

"Oh, great." Cindy groaned. "Dad's going to be suspended all year!"

"Not necessarily, if the state officials think the drugging was accidental," Dr. Smith said. But she didn't sound hopeful. "The officials haven't charged Ian yet. They sent out for a split-sample test and won't comment until the results are in."

"Well, someone could have thrown the heroin in Glory's stall to get rid of it if there was a drug bust," Ian said. "That points to a stable hand's doing this. I don't know how that fits with the procaine, but I'll find out if federal agents recently searched the stables." He smiled sadly. "I don't really have all that much to do now that I'm barred from training."

"This is crazy," Samantha said angrily.

Cindy pressed her face into Glory's satiny neck and closed her eyes. The colt's soft, warm fur tickled her cheek. He was healthy again now, but she was terrified for him. *We have to do something fast. Next time it could be a bigger dose.*

12

LATER THAT AFTERNOON CINDY LOOKED UP AT THE BIG TV screen hanging above the track snack bar. Matchless had just blazed between horses to take the lead in his allowance race! "Way to go, Matchless!" she cheered. "Go get 'em!" Cindy set her two bowls of nachos on the snack-bar counter and turned her full attention to the race.

Matchless stormed through the final quarter, dusting the competition in the stretch. He flashed under the wire to win his second race by four lengths. "Yes!" Cindy cried. *Another victory for Whitebrook!* she thought.

Matchless pranced to the winner's circle, with Chris Akron up, the colt's regular jockey. The colt obviously was aware he had done well. Cindy smiled as Matchless looked straight at the TV camera, as if he knew exactly what to do.

She saw the pride and relief on Mike's face as he

walked across the track to greet the horse and jockey. Cindy was so glad they'd won. In light of the drug scandal, everyone from Whitebrook needed a confidence boost.

"You know that horse?" the snack-bar attendant asked her. He had watched the race as closely as Cindy. The man was in his fifties and paunchy, but at one time he might have been a trainer or groom.

"Yes. Matchless is one of ours—a Whitebrook Farm horse," Cindy said proudly.

The older man nodded. "Good run."

I'm glad not everyone thinks Whitebrook horses win only because we drug them, Cindy thought. "Thanks." She smiled at the attendant and paid for the nachos and two sodas. Balancing the cardboard carton carefully, she walked back through the crowded snack bar and betting area to the shed row. Cindy planned to take the snacks to Glory's stall and share them with Max. Since they'd gotten the bad news about Glory and the morphine that afternoon, Cindy had refused to leave the colt. She'd come to buy the food only after Max had promised not to take his eyes off Glory for a nanosecond the whole ten minutes she was gone.

"I wish Sagebrush had run well," Cindy murmured as she wove among the hot-walkers, grooms, and trainers taking horses to and from the track. Sagebrush had gotten away from the gate clean and fast in his race earlier that day, but by midstretch the field had begun to draw off from him. He had come up empty at the wire and finished a dismal last in the field of twelve.

At least Matchless would go on to stakes races. After his excellent performance just now, that was what Mike probably had planned for him.

That would be great—the farm will have money again if we have a stakes winner, Cindy thought. *But of course Shining will be a stakes winner again once we solve the drugging mystery—whenever that is. Then Ashleigh will ride her the way she used to.*

In the stable yard in front of the Whitebrook shed row the track guards were gone, and a small crowd had gathered again. Cindy felt the now-familiar clutch of fear in her stomach. She tried to tell herself that the crowd was there only for the usual reason—they hoped to hear more bad news about Whitebrook horses.

"Designer drugs," Joe Gallagher said loudly. He was standing at the front of the crowd. Cindy realized that people had gathered to listen to him. "It wouldn't surprise me if those two horses Whitebrook ran today come up clean. But that's only because the tests can't pick up what they're using."

"Makes sense," called somebody in the crowd.

Cindy pushed through to the barn, her cheeks flaming. She thought the knot in her stomach might be permanent. *How can they think we would do something like that to our horses?* she wondered.

Len and Samantha were in the feed room, emptying sacks of grain. Cindy stuck her head through the doorway. She couldn't believe they weren't out there yelling back at the crowd. "Len, Sammy," she said. "Didn't you hear what they're saying outside?"

Samantha made a face. "We heard," she said. "We're just not going to dignify their accusations by giving them a response."

"Don't pay them any mind," Len said consolingly. "We know we run our horses clean, and soon everyone else will, too. Truth will out. Or everyone will finally forget about all this."

I don't really think so, Cindy thought, sitting on a full sack of grain. The previous night Samantha had told Cindy about a trainer whose horse had tested positive for isoxsuprine, the medication used to help circulation in horses' hooves. Dr. Smith was using it in Salutation, Cindy remembered. The trainer had denied any wrongdoing, but years later the story still kept cropping up to haunt him, Samantha had said.

Samantha folded a feed sack and placed it on a neat pile. "I could use a rest from the negative comments," she said. "People are saying the wildest things. I can't believe they think we drugged Glory all along—the tests would have picked it up. Or do they imagine we've got an underground laboratory where we spend half our lives designing undetectable drugs?"

"Guess so," said Len.

"Do they think Glory won his first race by twenty lengths because we drugged him?" Cindy asked angrily.

"I can't believe anyone really thinks drugs would improve a horse's performance to that degree," Samantha said. "We'd be stupid to try to get a horse to win by giving him drugs."

"Why?" Max asked, looking around the doorway to the feed room.

"Don't leave Glory alone," Cindy cautioned, jumping up and running to the door.

"He's not alone," Max said impatiently. "We're all right here."

"Cindy's right," Len said unexpectedly. "Let's move this party out to the aisle. It doesn't take but a second to give a horse an injection or throw something in his stall."

Glory tossed his head and gave welcoming nickers as they all approached him. He seemed to be saying, *The more, the merrier.*

"You're in a good mood," Cindy told him. "I wish you could talk. Then you could tell us what's going on and we wouldn't have to guess."

Cindy looked critically at Glory. Miraculously, he seemed to bear no ill effects from the morphine or heroin drugging. His gray coat was shining from the bath and brushing she'd given him earlier that afternoon, and his dark eyes were affectionate and contented. If her arms hadn't hurt so much and she hadn't been so tired, Cindy might have thought she'd imagined the whole thing.

Cindy dropped a kiss on Glory's nose, then joined Samantha on a hay bale placed just out of Glory's reach. Max and Len leaned against the wall opposite. Cindy wondered how long they would have to keep up their vigil. She just prayed the problem wouldn't follow them to Saratoga.

"Anyway, the reason no one in their right mind would give a racehorse drugs is that the pharmacologic effects of drugs are erratic," Samantha said. "It would be very tricky to stimulate a horse just right so that he would win

136

his race and not fall to pieces. You'd have to give the drug at the exact right time so that its effect peaked during the race, not before or after. If the horse peaked before, he'd be exhausted during the race, and obviously after's no good. Besides, because every horse responds differently to drugs, there'd be no way of guessing how Glory would respond to procaine or morphine unless we sat around every day giving him drugs and watching his response."

"Yeah, right," Max said. "I can really see you doing that."

Samantha frowned. "I guess that's why we're all so upset about these charges—they don't make sense, besides what the drugging is doing to Glory's career and health."

Samantha reached out and absently stroked Glory's nose. Shining craned her neck around her stall door and whinnied in obvious protest.

"No, Glory's not more important than you," Samantha said, getting up and going to her horse.

"I sure hope Matchless doesn't test positive," Cindy said. "Did you see his race?"

Len pointed to a small TV propped on a table. "Every bit."

"It's great news that he won," Cindy said.

"We were due to have a good day." Len nodded.

I guess this is a good day, Cindy thought. It would really have been a good one if the cloud of suspicion and scandal hadn't been hanging over Whitebrook.

"I'm worried about Sagebrush," Samantha said. "After a finish as bad as today's and in light of our drug problem, the officials will be sure to test him."

137

Cindy knew that the general rule at racetracks was to test all winners and any horse that ran badly. But every Whitebrook horse that had run since the scandal broke had ended up in the testing barn.

"Shining was okay after her last race," Cindy said.

"Yes, she was." Samantha sat back down on the hay bale. "Because of that, I'm hopeful Matchless and Sagebrush will come up negative. I think there's a good chance they will. Neither of them looked drugged today, the way Glory did when he worked before the track vets. Sagebrush probably just had an off day. Or he may not ever make it out of allowance company. Most horses aren't stakes caliber."

"So if just Glory tested positive, that's not so bad for Whitebrook, is it?" Cindy asked. It still hurt to say that Glory had been drugged. "Will the stewards go easier on Dad if only one horse got drugged?"

"Hard to say." Len shook his head. "Ian had a spotless record until now. But it's bad timing. The racing industry is on an antidrug campaign right now."

"Well, Cindy's right about one thing," Samantha said. "If just one horse tests positive, it won't look as if drugs are rampant in our stable."

"I can't imagine anyone would believe that, even if they do spread the story around," Len said. "What I'm wondering is if this whole business has to do with money."

"Another owner or trainer could drug someone else's horse to better their horses' chances," Samantha said. "Is that what you mean, Len?"

Len nodded. "If you knew a horse would be drugged, you definitely wouldn't bet on him, even if he went in as the favorite. You could make a lot of money."

"Are you talking about Flightful and Joe Gallagher?" Samantha asked.

"I'm not to the point of naming names," Len said. "Just wondering."

"Even if Joe Gallagher has a motive, he can't get in our barn—we've made sure of that." Samantha stood up, pushing back her red hair. "This is enough sitting around and speculating for me. I'm going to walk Shining and limber her up a little."

"I'd best get back to organizing the evening feed," Len said.

Cindy looked at Max. "I'm going to guard Glory."

"I'll stay with you for a while," Max said. "I guess my mom knows to look for me here. She'll probably be by soon to check on Glory and the other Whitebrook horses anyway."

Glory was gazing affectionately at Cindy from his stall. The expression in his big eyes was warm and trusting, the way it always was—except when he had been drugged.

Cindy looked at him sadly. She was glad Glory didn't understand what was going on—that he was at the center of a huge controversy. As far as he was concerned, as long as he felt all right and she was with him, there was no problem.

Tears filled Cindy's eyes. Glory was in disgrace, but it wasn't his fault. She took his head in her arms, pushing his thick forelock out of his eyes.

"He seems okay." Max patted Glory's neck.

"He's not, though." Cindy wiped away her tears. "He can't run. Even when the track vets clear him, he may not ever run as fast as he did before. And what if somebody drugs him again?"

"Let's try to figure this whole thing out," Max said.

"I've been trying forever." Cindy slumped against Glory's stall door. "We just have to, though. Heroin's one of the worst drugs I can think of. Whoever's doing this may kill Glory next time."

13

"START FROM THE BEGINNING AND LET'S GO OVER IT ALL again," Max said patiently.

"Okay." Cindy drew a deep breath and tried to collect her thoughts. "Let's go in the stall with Glory. I know it sounds crazy, but I feel better when I can see every inch of him."

"That doesn't sound crazy to me," Max said.

They sat next to each other on the straw in Glory's stall. Glory looked over at his two companions and grabbed a big bite of hay from his net. He seemed pleased to have so much company. A few strands of hay dropped in Cindy's lap.

"Thanks, Glory." Cindy laughed. "Are we in your house, and you're the host?"

Max took a strand of hay and twirled it between his fingers. "Let's go back to the first drug he got, the procaine," he said. "Penicillin is a drug a vet would use, or somebody around a vet."

"But how would they have given it to Glory? We've been watching him so closely," Cindy protested. "And the track's posted a twenty-four-hour guard on Glory now. No one can get near him for any reason except Whitebrook people and your mom and her assistant."

"Well, I don't think my mom is drugging Glory," Max said quickly.

"I didn't say she was." Cindy frowned in thought. "Somebody has it in for Glory. But who?"

"It does seem like it's just Glory, since Shining was okay after the Metropolitan," Max said.

"Nobody hates Glory except those horrible men who stole him last year." Cindy frowned. "But they're in jail."

"What worries me is that the person will probably try again with a bigger dose of heroin or something like fentanyl, a really powerful stimulant," Max said.

Cindy closed her eyes, feeling overwhelmed. She could hardly believe that a few days before, she'd thought she didn't have a care in the world about Glory. She'd thought he just had to get out on the track and win his races, and nothing could stop him from doing that.

"I still don't see how this happened," she said. "My dad, Ashleigh, Mike, and Len are really careful about who comes around Whitebrook and our stalls here. They'd notice if a stranger was wandering around with a hypodermic or a package of drugs."

"So it was an inside job," Max suggested.

"But who?" Cindy frowned.

"What about the Townsends?" Cindy had told Max

about Whitebrook's ongoing battles with them. "Couldn't they hang around the stable without anyone getting suspicious?" he asked.

Cindy shook her head. "I guess they could, but I can't see one of the Townsends doing something like this. Lavinia gave me a funny look the day Glory tested positive, but I think she was just glad Whitebrook is having trouble. Glory's not racing against any of the Townsends' star horses, so they're not mad at him. And if they got caught drugging a horse—"

"They'd go to jail," Max finished.

"Yeah, and they're so worried about appearances. Lavinia would never want to go to jail." Cindy yawned and shook her head. She probably hadn't gotten more than five hours of sleep a night for the past three nights.

"I heard Ashleigh say that Lavinia suggested running Mr. Wonderful on bute, even though his leg is sore," Max said.

"Yeah," Cindy agreed. "I didn't say Lavinia was nice. But she didn't dare suggest that to Ashleigh. Ashleigh found out from Len, who heard it from Hank, the head groom at Townsend Acres. Lavinia has messed up with the horses so much, no one takes her suggestions seriously anymore."

"I can see why." Max frowned. "She's practically killed every horse she had anything to do with."

"What Brad and Lavinia *are* doing is spreading it around that Glory has always been on drugs," Cindy said. "Yesterday I overheard a bunch of trainers and grooms saying that. Samantha thinks Brad and Lavinia are trying to discredit Whitebrook. They just can't stand Ashleigh."

"Okay." Max frowned with concentration. "So the Townsends didn't drug Glory, and neither did another owner or trainer, because they couldn't get to Glory. A stable hand would be more likely to have given him the heroin, but they can't get in here, either. So where does that leave us?" he asked.

"Nowhere." Cindy slumped back in the straw.

Glory stamped his foot. "Yes, I know you're bored, boy," Cindy said. "We'll go out for a walk tonight. I'm sorry you don't get to have much fun."

"Hey, I hear a horse coming," Max said.

Cindy sat up straight. "Matchless must be back from the testing barn," she said. "Let's go see him."

Mike and Ashleigh were leading the chestnut colt to his stall, opposite Shining's. Cindy thought Ashleigh looked better than she had in days. She didn't look nearly as tired, and she was smiling. "Here's our new star!" Ashleigh said.

Cindy walked alongside them. "You were fantastic, Matchless!" she praised, resting a hand on the colt's neck.

"He couldn't have run a better race," Ashleigh agreed.

The colt arched his neck and pranced a little, seeming to bask in the attention. Even Glory stuck his head over the stall door and gave Matchless an affectionate push on the rump as the other horse went by.

"More good news," Ashleigh said, unfolding a chair and sitting. "Sagebrush tested negative for drugs."

"The bad news is that the press is still on our case," Mike said. "They seem determined to make an example of us."

"I don't think it's only that." Ashleigh sighed. "Whitebrook had been doing so well—every horse we touched turned in golden performances. I suppose it's only human nature that people are enjoying our downfall."

Cindy frowned. It would be one thing if Whitebrook really had drugged its horses, she thought. But this wasn't fair.

"It can only go uphill from here," Mike said. "How's Glory?"

"He's okay." Cindy looked back at the colt just to make sure. Ashleigh, Mike, and everyone but Len had missed most of Glory's horrible reaction to the heroin because they'd been busy with Sagebrush. Cindy wasn't sure if she should tell them how sick Glory had been. It would just make them feel bad.

"Why don't you bring him out and we'll take a look?" Ashleigh suggested.

Cindy led the big gray horse into the aisle and walked him up and down. Glory really was breathtakingly beautiful, she thought. His dappled coat glittered as she guided him through a patch of sunlight near the barn door, and his step was springy and powerful. He looked every inch the racehorse. Cindy heard sighs of appreciation from the group.

"He couldn't look better, Cindy," Ashleigh said approvingly. "You really work magic with him."

"I'm glad none of the drugs has hurt him." Cindy frowned. "I mean, they don't seem to have."

"We won't really know that until he runs again," Mike said. "But if we can just keep him from getting drugged

145

again, I don't see why he can't run in a couple of weeks in the Brooklyn Handicap, the way we planned."

Cindy's heart thumped with excitement. So Glory's second stakes race was still on! "Glory, did you hear that?" Cindy said happily. "You're going to be running soon!"

Glory skittered sideways. Maybe she was scaring him a little, but it was good for him, Cindy thought. Soon he'd have to get used to all the commotion at the track again!

"We'll have to run him before the track vets," Mike said. "I think we can try again in a day or two and still have him ready for a stakes race in two weeks. We just have to hope our increased security measures work. I'll stay on as Glory's trainer until we get Ian's situation cleared up."

"I sure hope that happens soon," Ashleigh said. "The officials really may take a dim view of Glory's being given not one drug but two. Especially since one of them was almost certainly heroin, a drug that's illegal not only at the track but everywhere else. Ian, Beth, and Samantha are with the stewards right now, trying to sort this out."

"Flightful's entered in that next stakes you're planning to put Glory in," Len remarked. "I'd think Joe would watch out for Glory now, after his colt lost two races to ours. But Joe probably thinks Glory won't be running in it, after all that's happened."

"He's wrong," Cindy said firmly. "I know Glory can run in the race. He can't wait to get out on the track, can you, boy? He's sick of the stall and just walking around the barn."

"I say we go for it," Mike said. "Put all this behind us."

Cindy hugged Glory. This was the best news in the world. And Mike was right—no one was ever going to drug Glory again. Cindy vowed to make sure of that.

14

THAT NIGHT CINDY ARRANGED A BLANKET AND PILLOW IN Glory's stall. "Guess what, boy—you're going to have company," she said. Cindy had finally worn her parents down, and they were letting her sleep there that night.

Glory nosed the pillow cautiously, then flipped it over. He backed up, snorting in surprise.

Cindy laughed. "It's just a pillow, Glory. You don't need one of those to sleep. But I sure will in here." She lay down to test out her bed and grimaced. The straw scratched, and it formed weird lumps under different parts of her back. *I don't care how uncomfortable it is. I'm staying,* she thought.

Beth looked over the stall door. "Sweet dreams," she said. "Honey, how are you going to get any sleep in there?"

"I don't know." Cindy looked up at Glory. He was looming over her, pushing at the pillow again. He might want to play most of the night, Cindy realized. Glory didn't need nearly as much sleep as she did.

Cindy smiled and reached up to stroke his silken neck. It would be fun anyway to spend the whole night with her horse. She sat up and looked over at Beth. "It doesn't matter if I don't get any sleep. You know I can't sleep in the motel either." Cindy decided not to tell Beth now that she intended to stay with Glory in the stall through his next stakes race—and after, if she had to.

Beth sighed. "Well, probably none of us will get much sleep until we get to the bottom of this."

Ian looked over the stall door. "Are you all set, Cindy?" he asked.

"Yup." Cindy examined her bedding and began pulling straw from under the blanket, trying to smooth out the lumps.

"Don't you want a cot?" Beth asked. "The ground is so hard."

"The straw's pretty soft, really." Glory would have a lot of fun playing with a cot, Cindy thought. He would probably knock it over or shake it all night. If she had to keep this up, she might consider a foam mattress, though. "Glory, let go!" she cried. The gray horse had the edge of her blanket between his teeth. With a quick yank he pulled it to his side of the stall and dropped it.

"Glory!" Cindy grabbed back the blanket. She was going to have to wrap it around herself to stop him from stealing it. If Glory kept up these games, she might get even less sleep than she thought. But maybe he would settle down when everyone else left.

Ian handed Cindy his cellular phone. "Call us if you need anything. Len will be sleeping on a cot in the feed room, and the track has stationed two guards outside." He hesitated. "Honey, staying out here is kind of a crazy idea. I can't imagine what could happen, but be very careful."

"I will." Staying in the stall might be crazy, Cindy thought, but she was happy for the first time in days. At least that night she could be sure nothing bad would happen to Glory.

Ian ran a hand through his auburn hair. "I really think the worst is over with Glory, Cindy, now that we're watching him so closely. He'll work before the track officials in two days and then move on to racing again."

Cindy nodded. "But I need to be here."

"Well, good night, then," Beth said. "We'll miss you."

"I'll be fine," Cindy assured them.

"See you first thing tomorrow morning," Ian said, still looking uncertain.

Cindy hung over the stall door and waved as her parents left. *So this is how Glory sees things,* she thought. *Tonight it's almost like I'm a horse. Neat!*

Cindy turned to Glory, who was gently nosing her back pockets. "Well, here we are, boy. Now what should we do?" The barn was almost completely silent. Cindy opened the stall door and wandered down the aisle. She hadn't visited the other Whitebrook horses yet that night. That should be her first priority.

Shining was asleep at the back of her stall. In the faint light her red-and-white coat looked a deep maroon. Cindy tiptoed by the stall so as not to disturb her. She'd expected to find Shining asleep, because the roan mare usually dozed early at night. Shining probably wasn't too tired—Samantha and Mike were only lightly working her while they decided whether to race her in the Suburban Handicap in July or the Whitney at Saratoga in August. Cindy hoped Glory would be able to run and do well again, making the decision easier for them.

She moved on to Sagebrush. The chestnut colt peered out of the stall at her, blowing in surprise. "It's okay," Cindy said, reaching out slowly to rub his blaze. "I'm just guarding." Sagebrush had turned out to have a bone chip in his knee and would need surgery. At least drugs weren't his problem, Cindy thought. The injury wasn't too bad. He might be able to race the next year as a three-year-old.

A soft thump at the far end of the barn startled her out of her thoughts. "Len?" Cindy called. She walked slowly toward the sound, peering through the shadows.

She could barely see the far end of the barn. The aisle was almost completely dark, except for spreading circles of dim yellow light from the overhead bulbs. Cindy glanced around nervously. Suddenly she realized there were a lot of places someone could hide in the barn—in one of the several empty stalls or behind a stack of straw or hay. If someone was already in there, they wouldn't have to get by the guards or Len.

Cindy glanced at Glory. He was looking in the direction of the noise, his ears pricked. So he had heard something strange, too.

Cindy tiptoed by the feed room. She was scared, but

she reminded herself that the track guards were just outside the barn. In the feed room she could hear Len snoring. He definitely hadn't been walking around.

"So what was that noise?" she whispered. Then she saw an upended bale of straw. It had just fallen off a stack of bales. Cindy smiled with relief. *So now I'm scared of falling straw. I really am jumpy,* she thought.

Cindy walked back to Glory's stall. The gray horse was eyeing her over the door, tossing his head. "Ready for some company, boy?" she asked. "Let's hear some music." Cindy brought her portable CD player into the stall and turned it to a low volume. One of her favorite songs filled the stall.

Glory lowered his head and half closed his eyes. "You like that song, too?" Cindy said with a smile. She straightened her blanket and pillow, then lay back and put her arms behind her head.

I always wanted to spend the night in Glory's stall, and here I am, she thought. *I just wish I weren't doing it because he's in so much danger.*

The minutes dragged on. A breeze touched the stable lights, making the shadows flicker and dance. *Actually, staying in the stable isn't so much fun,* Cindy thought. She felt afraid, even though she couldn't put her finger on why. The barn seemed full of a silent, growing menace.

Cindy shook her head. "Nobody's in here," she said firmly. She reached her hand out to Glory. The big horse stepped close to her and touched her fingertips with his muzzle. "Good boy," Cindy said softly. "We'll be okay together."

Maybe the barn felt so creepy just because it was late at night, she thought. Or maybe it was because of what had been happening there. Cindy looked up at the black hole that was the space above Glory's half door. Somebody's hand had thrust the heroin through there recently. Whose hand had it been?

She shivered. Glory moved uneasily around the stall. Either he was picking up on her mood or something was bothering him also.

"What is it, Glory?" Cindy murmured. "Why are we scared? I was never scared in the stable before."

Glory gently touched his nose to her hair and inhaled deeply. Cindy looked up at her horse, feeling so much love for him she thought she might burst. "I'm here, boy," she said. "I promise I won't let anything happen to you."

Cindy took a deep breath and leaned back. She needed distraction. "Okay, let's think one more time about who did this," she said. "A stranger couldn't have gotten in here. The only people who can are everyone at Whitebrook and the Smiths. But nobody at Whitebrook is going to drug one of our own horses—I know them too well. I don't know Max and his mother as well, but it's not them. That would be too crazy."

Glory snorted uneasily. Cindy reached up a hand to soothe him. "So that leaves nobody, right, boy? Or . . . wait." Cindy's eyes widened. "I forgot. Jim Trewell?"

Maybe that's who it was, she thought excitedly. She remembered how Jim had been the last out of the barn at Whitebrook the time she'd gone on rounds with Dr.

153

Smith. With Dr. Smith, Jim was constantly in and out of the Whitebrook barns at home and here at the track.

Finally Cindy had a new angle on the mystery. But then she shook her head. "Why would Jim do it?" Cindy said aloud. "The drugging is making Dr. Smith look bad, because the people who don't think Whitebrook is drugging Glory think Dr. Smith is, either on purpose or because she's careless. Jim wouldn't want that because Dr. Smith is his boss."

But I don't know Jim the way I do all the other people who can get close to Glory, Cindy thought. *He's really the only possibility.* She chewed her thumbnail. "I still want to check him out, but how?" she asked Glory.

Hearing her voice had made Glory relax. He made another foray at her blanket.

"Stop it, you." Cindy snatched the blanket away again. "Hey, I know! I'll call Max. He can tell me more about Jim."

Keeping a careful eye on Glory, Cindy punched in the motel number on her dad's phone. At the last second she almost hung up. What if she was wrong and Max told her she was crazy? But she didn't think he would.

"Hello?" Max answered on the second ring.

"It's me. I'm in Glory's stall."

"What are you doing there?" Max asked. He sounded so alert, Cindy was sure he'd been awake as well.

"I'm watching Glory," she said. "Len's sleeping in the feed room and the track guards are outside, but I don't want to leave Glory alone. If I'm here, I can make sure he doesn't get drugged again."

"Makes sense to me," Max said.

Cindy smiled. Max didn't think she was silly for sleeping in a stall. He understood right away why she had to do it.

"I wanted to ask you something," she said. "What do you know about Jim Trewell?"

"That he's a top veterinary student," Max answered. "He got all A's in vet school. My mom hired him about a month ago. She said he had great references."

"I just wondered . . . Can your mom find out more about him?"

Max was silent for a second. "Oh, I follow you," he said. "You think Jim may have drugged Glory."

"Well . . . I don't know." Cindy hated to accuse someone without any proof. It wasn't fair, and she had a feeling she could get in real trouble doing that. Jim certainly wouldn't appreciate it.

"I'll ask my mom right now," Max said quickly. "She's still up."

"Join the club."

"Can't sleep, huh?" Max said sympathetically. "I could come over and keep you company."

"Will your mom let you?" Cindy remembered her parents' resistance to the idea.

"Oh, sure," Max said. "Sometimes she sleeps in stalls with really sick horses. I'll be over in fifteen minutes. My mom will bring me."

"Great!" Cindy clicked off the phone. She was glad she'd have company. She tried not to think that the reason she and Max were staying with Glory in his stall was the same reason Dr. Smith stayed with horses—because Glory's life was in danger.

Cindy had almost dozed off when Max arrived. "Hey, wake up," he said, tossing a sleeping bag and pillow into the corner of the stall opposite hers.

Cindy sat up with a jerk. "Sorry," she mumbled. She could feel straw tickling her back. Glory nickered and stepped to the stall door to greet their guest.

"Hi, Glory." Max patted Glory's neck. "He doesn't look drugged, does he?"

"No." Cindy sighed, trying to comb straw out of her hair. "I don't think he is now—he seems perfectly fine. I just hope the drugs he already got didn't hurt him. Whatever makes him such a great runner might be gone. I feel sick when I think about that. I sure don't want to risk his getting any more drugs."

"I bet he's okay," Max said confidently. "We'd know if the drugs did something to him. He looks the same as ever."

"He does to me, too." Cindy reached up to rub one of Glory's slender, straight legs.

"I asked my mom about Jim," Max said, sitting next to her on her blanket. "She's going to check up on him."

"So she didn't think we're dumb for suspecting him?"

"Nope. She doesn't know Jim that well, either—except professionally."

"I hope it isn't Jim," Cindy said. "I mean, for your mom's sake."

"She wouldn't be too happy if she'd hired somebody like that," Max agreed. "She's doing a little checking about his employment and vet school records on her computer tonight, but I guess she won't know much until morning." Max reached into his denim jacket and pulled out a deck of cards. "Want to play gin rummy?"

"What would we play for?" Cindy smiled. She felt a lot better now that Max was there.

"Let's bet straw!"

Cindy giggled. "We have plenty of that!"

Max dealt the cards and they began to play. The stable was still, except for the soft sighs of sleeping or relaxing horses. The only real interruption to the peace and quiet was from Glory. Every few minutes he would wander over and try to eat their straw chips off the blanket.

"Glory, it's just straw—it's not good to eat!" Cindy laughed.

Glory lipped up a few more strands. He seemed to be saying, *If you think this stuff is so important, it must be good to eat.*

"Maybe we should deal Glory in." Max grinned.

"Maybe." Cindy grinned back. "Or he could play for you—I think you're losing."

"Glory just ate half my chips," Max protested.

"Sure, sure, a likely story." Cindy dealt the cards again with a flourish. She decided she liked this game. "Have you heard from anybody back home?" she asked.

"Nope—nothing." Max studied his cards. "Have you?"

"I got a letter from Mandy a little while ago, and I finally got one from Heather," Cindy said. "It was really short, though."

"What did she say?"

"Just that it's rained a lot, and that she's trying to keep

up with Mandy. Mandy wants to go swimming every day, rain or shine, because the doctor said it will strengthen her legs."

"I don't know Mandy," Max said.

"Oh, right. I just assumed everybody did. She's really something." Cindy explained a little about Mandy's jumping lessons and her disability.

"Maybe I'll look up Heather when I go home and meet Mandy," Max said, spreading his hand of cards. "I'd like to watch some jumping at Tor's this summer."

"Aren't you going to Saratoga?" Cindy asked.

"No—we have to get back to Lexington. My mom's Kentucky clients are screaming."

Cindy felt a flash of disappointment and worry. She'd been having so much fun with Max. And he'd been such a big help with Glory now that all these disasters had happened. "That's too bad," she said.

"Yeah, I like Saratoga. Are you coming home anytime before the end of summer?" Max asked.

"I'm not sure. I might be able to come once. My dad and Mike have to go back to get Sierra and a couple of other horses they're running at Saratoga. But I can't leave Glory until we get things straightened out with him." Cindy noticed that the big gray horse had finally tired of gin rummy and fallen asleep. He was standing on three legs with his eyes closed, breathing deeply.

Cindy looked back at her hand of cards. "Gin," she said, reaching for Max's chips.

Max groaned and gathered the cards. "Who's going to be in the field for Glory's next race?" he asked.

"A lot of good horses so far. They've all won stakes races against pretty stiff competition. The one to beat will be Flightful, though." Cindy yawned. "He's the only horse who's ever even challenged Glory. I think Glory can go on beating him—if Glory's really okay, if the drugs haven't done anything to him. And if I can stop him from getting any more drugs."

"Let's try to get some sleep," Max said. "Maybe my mom will turn up something on Jim by tomorrow."

"Yeah." Cindy couldn't stop yawning. She wondered how long she could keep up her vigil over Glory. She was already exhausted, but she didn't intend to leave the stall in the daytime, either.

Oh, well, I'll just keep living the way Glory does, she said to herself, looking fondly over at the dozing horse. *I guess if he can do it, I can, too—as long as somebody brings me food.*

Max had fallen asleep. He was curled up in his sleeping bag on the other side of Glory.

Cindy smiled, then closed her eyes contentedly. *Max is the best friend I ever had,* she thought as she drifted off to sleep.

15

CINDY WOKE WITH A JOLT AND SAT UP STRAIGHT, RUBBING HER eyes. From the quiet, heavy feel of the night Cindy could tell that it was very late, but she didn't think she'd been asleep long. *I bet it's about three A.M.* She got up to check on Glory.

Glory moved a little at the back of the stall. Cindy couldn't tell if he was sleeping or not, but she could see that his ears were relaxed. *Good, he isn't scared,* she thought. Then she realized Glory was awake. He was moving to the door.

"What is it, boy?" she whispered.

Glory whickered, as if he were greeting a friend. Cindy looked to see who it was—and saw a black-gloved hand with a hypodermic poised above Glory's neck.

"No!" Cindy tried to scream, but her voice came out as a croak. She rushed at Glory, her hands outstretched to block the shot. In her panic Cindy didn't think what could happen to her if she was injected with a shot at the strength meant for a horse. She only knew that no one was going to hurt Glory while she could do the slightest thing about it. She was dimly aware that Max had run to the stall door as well.

Suddenly the hypodermic was withdrawn. Glory jumped away and stood snorting at the back of the stall. With a shuddering gasp, Cindy looked up at the intruder.

"It's just me, Cindy—calm down," Jim said.

Cindy stared into his face. "Jim! What are you doing?" she asked. Jim looked as startled as she was. Cindy's heart was still hammering. But Jim didn't look sinister anymore. He looked the way he always did—calm, competent, and irritated with her.

"Shhh, don't upset the horse," Jim whispered. He quickly capped the hypodermic and replaced it in his medical bag.

"What was in that?" Cindy asked. Glory had recovered from his spook and returned to the stall door. Cindy tried to push him away without taking her eyes off Jim. But Glory didn't want to go—the little sleep he'd had seemed to have put him in a party mood. He playfully pushed Cindy back on the seat of her jeans and stayed where he was.

"It's just a tranquilizer," Jim explained. "Glory hasn't been getting enough sleep."

"Then why don't you give it to him?" Max asked suspiciously.

"Well, I didn't know you two were here." Jim shrugged

and glanced down the aisle. "He'll probably sleep all right if he has company."

Cindy hesitated. She almost believed Jim, but not quite. "If Dr. Smith ordered the shot, why didn't she tell us you'd be coming over?" she asked.

"We just talked about it a few minutes ago," Jim said, picking up his bag. "See you in the morning."

"Wait," Max said sharply. "I'm going to call my mom. I don't think she prescribed a tranquilizer for Glory at three in the morning without telling us." Max stared hard at Jim. "I want to know what's really in that hypodermic."

Jim's face changed in a second. He looked so menacing, Cindy backed away from the stall door with a cry. Glory, sensing the change in atmosphere, jumped back, too.

"Don't try to push me around, kid," Jim said. "You want to know what's in there?" He removed the syringe from his bag again. "Well, take a look!"

Jim loomed above them, raising the hypodermic. His face was twisted with rage. For a second Cindy was terrified he was going to stab Max with it. Now there was no question in Cindy's mind that Jim had done the drugging.

"Len, help!" she shouted. "Somebody!"

"Hold it right there, buddy," one of the track guards called from the end of the aisle. "Put down the hypodermic nice and slow." Len ran out of the feed room to join them.

Jim glared at the guards. Then he threw the hypodermic to the barn floor. It shattered into a million

162

glistening pieces. The liquid that had been inside it formed a small, lethal-looking pool. The guards ran over and seized Jim's arms.

"Are you all right?" Len asked Max and Cindy, hurrying up to them. He put an arm around each of them. "That sure was close!"

"We're fine." Cindy was glad for the reassuring warmth of Len's arm. Her hands were shaking, and even her teeth were chattering. She couldn't take her eyes off the dark, sinister pool of spilled liquid that had been in the hypodermic. Glory and Max had come so close to being stabbed with that. Cindy didn't know what it was yet, but she was sure it would have made them very sick.

Len jerked a thumb at Jim. "What made him think he could get away with this?" he asked the guards. "Where were you people?"

"A groom told us a horse had just been drugged in another barn and we left to check it out," one of the guards said. "But when we got there, the groom had disappeared and the night watchman had no idea what we were talking about. It was a hoax."

"Did you see who that 'groom' was?" Len asked.

The guard shook his head. "Too dark." He handcuffed Jim and the two guards walked him down the aisle.

"Why did you do it?" Max yelled after him. "Why?"

Jim looked back. He seemed calm again. "Why don't you ask her?" he said, nodding at Cindy.

"Come on, that's enough for tonight." One of the track guards roughly shouldered Jim toward a waiting van.

Cindy sank down in Glory's stall. Now that the

excitement was wearing off, her knees wouldn't hold her. "What did Jim mean?" she asked. "What have I got to do with this?"

"I think I can answer that," Dr. Smith said, looking over the stall door. "Thank God you two are in one piece."

"Jim was serious?" Cindy looked up in astonishment. Of all the theories they'd had about why someone had drugged Glory, the possibility that she was the target had never occurred to anyone.

"You were the beginning of it all," Dr. Smith said. "One of the men who stole Glory last year is Jim's father."

"What?" Cindy gasped.

Dr. Smith nodded. "Jim used his mother's last name so that no one would make the connection. But that's what drew his attention to Glory. He knew who you were, Cindy, from the newspaper article that recently came out about you two. The minute I found out Jim's full last name from the vet school records, I drove over here. I realized that you, Max, and Glory were in real danger."

Cindy shuddered, remembering the hypodermic so close to her friend and beloved horse.

"Mom, what is that?" Max asked, pointing to the shiny spilled liquid. "That was in the hypodermic Jim was about to give Glory."

Dr. Smith pulled on gloves and scooped some of the spilled liquid into a small vial. Very cautiously she sniffed it. "I think I know," she said. "But I'll tell you tomorrow when I'm sure. It's not good—I can tell you that much."

"Cindy!" Ian and Beth rushed up to Glory's stall. Close

164

behind them were Samantha, Ashleigh, and Mike. Beth and Ian let themselves into the stall and hugged Cindy as if they never meant to let her go.

"So I guess you had a little excitement," Ashleigh said. Her hazel eyes were filled with concern.

Cindy managed a weak laugh. "A little. Did you hear about Jim?"

"Yes, we just talked to the guards. Jim's saying he only did this to get even with you, Cindy, for sending his father to jail," Samantha said.

"I think Jim is insane." Cindy turned to Glory and ran her fingers down his dappled neck. He was safe, she told herself again. Finally the nightmare was over. "Oh, boy," she said, throwing her arms around him. "Everything's okay now. No one's going to hurt you ever again."

"So you can come home to sleep," Ian said. "All clear."

Cindy brushed off her jeans and glanced out the barn door. The dark gray light of dawn tinged the sky. *Wow, I stayed up all night. I don't think I ever did that before,* she thought. She looked back at Glory. The first light was turning him a darker shade of gray, almost blue.

Cindy dropped her head against Glory's neck. They'd been through so much the past few days. Now the danger was over, but she still needed to be with him a little longer.

The big gray horse looked back at her, his eyes soft. "I think I'll stay here," she said to her parents. "Just for the rest of tonight."

"Okay, sweetie," Ian said with a sigh. "Somehow I was sure that's what you were going to do."

"Well, now we know the whole story," Dr. Smith said the next morning as she walked up to Cindy with Ashleigh, Mike, Samantha, and Max.

Cindy was grazing Glory just outside the barn. The gray horse almost glowed with health and good conditioning in the strong morning sun. But the heat wasn't bothering Glory a bit that day, Cindy noted with satisfaction. He didn't have a mark of sweat on him. That more than made up for how tired she still felt. She hadn't gotten much sleep in the stall, and at six she'd been woken up for good when Len and Mike began taking the horses out to the track. "What *is* the whole story?" she asked. "Did you find out more about Jim?"

"We sure did," Samantha said. "It turns out Jim and Joe Gallagher are old buddies."

"Before Jim joined me, he worked briefly for the vet who treats a number of Joe's horses," Dr. Smith said.

Cindy looked from one face to another. "So Joe was involved in this?"

"Very." Ashleigh nodded. "It all boils down to money."

"Len was right," Cindy murmured.

"Jim has a lot of debts from vet school," Dr. Smith said. "That initially made the idea of making some easy money attractive to him. He and Joe decided to fix Glory's first race at Belmont by drugging Glory with procaine. Jim administered the procaine to him right before he was shipped to the track, on our last visit to Whitebrook. That way Glory stood a good chance of testing positive."

"And it was easier to give Glory the procaine at Whitebrook," Mike added. "Our security isn't as tight at home as it is at the track, with so many strangers around."

"Glory was favored to win his race," Samantha said. "But Jim and Joe knew that he wouldn't, because they'd drugged him and he would be disqualified. That gave Flightful a much better chance of winning. Jim and Joe determined the outcome of the race ahead of time."

"They must have bet a bundle on Flightful," Mike added.

"Why did they give Glory heroin?" Cindy asked. She looked quickly over at him. The gray horse had his muzzle immersed nearly to his eyes in a small patch of clover. There was absolutely no sign now that he had been given such a horrible drug, she thought with relief.

"To throw suspicion off Jim," Dr. Smith said. "That made it look as if a stable hand were doing the drugging."

"They also hoped that with the situation so muddled, we wouldn't chance running Glory in his next stakes race," Ashleigh added. "That would definitely improve the odds for Flightful to win."

"Money again," Cindy said. She couldn't believe people would actually hurt a horse to make money.

"Joe must have found out that we did plan to run Glory after all," Ashleigh said. "He and Jim couldn't keep drugging Glory, because eventually they'd get caught. The track officials were starting to think something very weird was going on and were about to launch their own investigation."

"I think Joe is a good enough trainer to realize that Glory may always beat his horse," Mike said. "That could be hard for him to accept, because Flightful is an extraordinary horse, too. It's just bad luck for Joe that Flightful came along at the same time Glory is racing."

"So Jim showed up at Glory's stall with a hypodermic," Cindy said. "What was in it?"

Dr. Smith looked at her. "Sodium pentobarbital," she said tersely.

"That's what you used to put down that old horse, Alice. Jim was going to kill Glory!" Cindy could barely take it in. She felt a shudder run through her entire body.

"Jim agreed to kill Glory for a share of Flightful's future winnings," Samantha said.

Dr. Smith sighed. "I feel responsible for this. Jim used my credentials and reputation to get close to Glory. He was allowed in the barns at all hours only because he was working for me."

"Jim is trying to say that he did this because his father is having such a hard time in prison," Samantha said.

Mike snorted. "Give me a break."

Ashleigh shrugged. "I guess that's why he made that comment to Cindy—the start of this whole thing was Jim's father going to jail."

"I think Jim is trying to give himself a much nobler motive than was really the case," Dr. Smith said.

"There's no reason ever to murder Glory or any other horse," Cindy said angrily. She couldn't begin to imagine how bare and sad her life would be without him.

"But I do think Jim got in over his head," Dr. Smith said. "He's young. I'm not sure he understood the consequences of his actions."

"I think this was all Joe's idea," Mike agreed.

"What's going to happen to them?" Cindy asked.

"It's going to be hard to prove Joe's involvement," Ashleigh said. "It's just Jim's word against his, and Jim doesn't have any proof."

"So they're going to get away with it?" Cindy asked in amazement.

"Joe probably is," Mike answered. "Jim will go to jail, or at least he won't be allowed to practice as a vet."

"But Joe's not going to get out of this scot-free," Ashleigh said determinedly. "We'll keep an eye on him."

"I wouldn't mind sleeping in Glory's stall for the rest of the meet," Cindy said. She wondered what would be the best way to tell her parents.

Ashleigh laughed. "Cindy, I don't think that will be necessary! We've caught the crooks."

"But there might be more. Glory's so—" Cindy hesitated. "He's just so special," she said. "He's going to do so well on the track. Won't people always want to stop him?"

Ashleigh put her arm around Cindy's shoulders. "I think very few people will. Most people are in racing because they love horses and their brilliant performances on the track. I think almost everyone will be with us all the way as Glory heads toward greatness."

And he will, Cindy thought, smiling as she watched the gray horse energetically crop the grass. *There's absolutely no doubt about that now.*

"Come on, Glory—let's go back up to the barn," she said. "You're not out to pasture anymore—we've got to start getting that coat extra shiny for race day."

16

TWO WEEKS LATER CINDY UNCLIPPED GLORY FROM THE crossties and took a last, critical look at him. It was time to lead the stallion down to the saddling paddock in preparation for the grade-two Brooklyn Handicap that afternoon.

A lot had happened since the night Jim had almost killed Glory, Cindy thought. Jim was out on bail, pending trial, but he had been banned for life from the Belmont track. No charges had been brought against Joe, for lack of evidence. Joe's reputation in horse circles, though, was definitely tarnished. The charges against Ian had been dropped almost immediately after Jim was caught, and the next day track veterinarians okayed Glory to run. In the past two weeks Ashleigh had brought Glory beautifully up to form on the track.

Glory looks so gorgeous, Cindy thought proudly. His coat had a soft sheen, and his muscles rippled from his neck to his hindquarters. The colt strained against the lead and nodded his elegant head, as if he was impatient to get going.

"Ready?" Len asked, coming up to them. His weathered face split in a smile. "So our big boy's returning to racing. This sure is a happy day."

"The best." Cindy gave Glory's long black-and-gray tail a last quick swipe with a brush. Flutters of nervousness and excitement were starting in her stomach. She told herself there was no need for that. This race would go well—the way Glory's races always had before the drugging scandal began.

Len and Cindy expertly guided Glory through the crowded backside. Dozens of sleek, highly conditioned Thoroughbreds were being prepared for races and returning from the track. Grooms brushed and carefully bandaged horses' legs in colorful wraps, while trainers called out orders and checked over the horses. Some horses walking to cool out were sheeted to their eyes against the chill of the day.

Cindy inhaled deeply. It had rained the night before, washing the smog out of the air and dissipating the long heat wave. The afternoon was fresh and cool, with a bright yellow sun and just a few clean-edged, wispy clouds in the sky.

"It's nice to be going to a race instead of sitting in Glory's stall," she said.

"Isn't that the truth," Len answered. "We're taking this horse back where he belongs."

"Len, good to see Glory again!" called a trainer Cindy

171

recognized from meets at Churchill Downs. Several other trainers and grooms called out good wishes, too.

Glory arched his neck and pranced in place, as if he were performing for his audience. Cindy gripped his lead rope tightly. "Look, there's Joe!" she whispered to Len.

"I saw him," Len said coldly. "He's not getting within ten yards of our horse."

Joe nodded stiffly as they passed. Len ignored him. "I'm usually fairly forgiving with people," he said. "But what Joe Gallagher did goes beyond the pale."

"It sure does!" Cindy certainly agreed with that.

Glory danced at the end of the lead, showing his usual high spirits. "Yes, you're a wonderful boy," Cindy said, patting his shoulder. "Nobody has any doubt about it now." The press was playing up Glory's story big time again, and Cindy was back in the limelight. She already had a lot of newspaper clippings from the New York papers to show Heather and Mandy.

"Here's our star horse," Ashleigh greeted them in the saddling paddock. Len quickly saddled Glory. The colt stood quietly, as if to prove that he was himself again.

"Do you feel okay?" Cindy asked Ashleigh with a worried frown. Just the previous day Ashleigh had been complaining of nausea and headaches.

"Never better." Ashleigh smiled. "I'm fine, Cindy. I've got some wonderful news to share soon."

What could that be? Cindy wondered. Ashleigh's eyes were sparkling, and her color was good. She looked great. *That's a big relief,* Cindy thought.

Ashleigh lightly sprang into the saddle as Len gave her a leg up.

"How does Glory seem to you?" Cindy asked. She was still afraid that Jim had hurt Glory with an undetectable drug. They might never know everything he had really given to the colt.

"Like himself," Ashleigh said. "Don't worry, Cindy. He's magnificent."

Cindy briskly patted Glory's neck. "I know. Get out there and win, boy—you can do it."

"See you in the winner's circle." Ashleigh winked and gathered her reins. Glory stepped off confidently.

"I'll be back in the barn," Len said to Cindy. "You better believe I'll have my eye on the TV."

Cindy nodded. "I'm going up to the stands."

As she darted through the crowds, Cindy noticed that the track was listed as fast. In a way, that was too bad, she thought. The horses were less likely to slip and fall on a fast track than on a muddy or sloppy one. But Glory was a "mudder"—he did well running through mud. A fast track evened the odds for him.

"Hey!" Max called.

Cindy whirled. Max was jogging after her. He stopped beside her, panting. "You're almost as fast as the horses here," he joked.

Cindy giggled. These days she and Max were best friends. Cindy knew she would never forget the way he had defended Glory with her against the worst danger of her horse's life. "Let's go up and watch the post parade," she said.

"I wouldn't miss it," Max answered as they made their way through the jostling, cheerful spectators. "Did you see that Flightful's going off as the favorite?"

"Yeah." Cindy knew that was probably because of the lingering question over Glory's health. *Well, most people don't know him like we do,* she thought. *I know he's going to win!*

"How did Glory look?" Ian asked Cindy as she and Max sat beside him in the stands.

"Like a champ." Cindy nodded confidently. Glory walked out onto the track, the first horse in the post parade. He lifted his head, sniffing. Cindy's heart swelled as she watched the beautiful colt step forward. At Ashleigh's signal he instantly broke into an easy, graceful trot.

Cindy turned her gaze to the rest of the field. Strike by Lightning, a dark bay, would be one to watch, she thought. Like Glory, he was a three-year-old, a seasoned pro who could be depended on to put in a strong effort. The top jockey this year was up on him. Thunder Squall, a gray four-year-old, was just in from California. He was known more as a sprinter, but he had placed second a few times in races over a mile.

Ashleigh rode Glory past Adieu, a French horse who had recently notched his first American stakes victory at Belmont. *He must like the track,* Cindy thought.

Flightful, under Felipe Aragon, was completing his warm-ups. The black colt looked powerful and relaxed, the way he always did.

"Glory's the best horse in the field, but those other horses aren't slouches," Max said.

"No, they're not," Cindy agreed. "Glory will have to be on his toes to win today." She focused her binoculars on the gate, where the horses were starting to be loaded. Glory went in third, next to Flightful, who was in the number-two hole. Ashleigh was tugging on her right rein to straighten Glory out.

The gate slammed open with a clang. Glory jumped out with a huge bound, but he stumbled. Cindy gasped. "Steady, boy!" she cried. She and Max exchanged a quick glance of horror.

The rest of the field roared up the stretch, their jockeys quickly maneuvering for position, but Glory couldn't find his stride. Ashleigh was desperately trying to steady him with her hands and legs.

"That was a terrible break from the gate!" Samantha shouted, leaning around Ian.

"I guess it was bound to happen sometime." Mike groaned. "I think Glory's out of the race—the field's got fifteen lengths on him. I'm just glad Ashleigh didn't take a spill."

He's fifteen lengths behind, but not for long! Cindy thought with growing excitement as she stared out at the track. Glory had finally gathered his legs under him and was starting to pick off the horses in front. Soon he was seventh in the ten-horse field, then fifth. Flightful had a four-length lead over Thunder Squall and an eight-length lead over Adieu, but Glory was steadily gaining on all the front-runners.

Cindy jumped to her feet, clenching her fists. *Go on, Glory!* she willed him. *You can do this!*

"I don't believe it," Samantha said, focusing her binoculars as the horses pounded down the backstretch. "Glory's coming back!"

Cindy looked through her own binoculars at the distant horses. Glory was running fast now, but he had a lot of ground to make up. Adieu and Thunder Squall had faded—now the race was down to Glory and Flightful.

The horses rounded the turn. "And it's March to Glory in second," the announcer called. "He's four lengths off the lead behind Flightful as they come into the stretch!"

"Go, Glory!" Cindy shrieked. Glory still trailed Flightful by four lengths as the two horses pounded through the last eighth of a mile. It would take a tremendous effort for the gray colt to catch Flightful now. Cindy had no idea if it was even possible for a horse to run as fast as Glory would have to in order to win.

Glory drew even with Flightful's flank. Then the horses were neck and neck.

"He's doing it!" Max yelled.

Flightful's jockey went for his whip, but Glory had his nose in front and clearly intended to keep it there. He opened up a one-length lead, then two lengths.

"And March to Glory's furious stretch drive has boldly carried him to the lead!" the announcer cried.

Cindy was dimly aware that she was screaming until her throat hurt and punching the air with her fists. She knew that no horse was going to catch Glory that day.

"He's scorching the track!" Ian said excitedly.

The roar of the crowd was deafening as the horses hurled toward the wire. Cindy put her hands to her mouth. She'd never seen Glory extend so far when he ran—his head was at the same level as his tail. He was showing so much heart!

"Watch this horse very carefully, ladies and gentlemen," the announcer sputtered. "You're seeing the next Just Victory here— I'll stake my reputation on it! But this is very disappointing for Flightful."

"Run, Glory!" Cindy screamed. "Oh, boy, you're the greatest horse in the world!"

The gray colt threw up his head as if he heard her. Then he changed leads and dug in, powering for the wire and victory. *There's no stopping him now—and there never will be!* Cindy thought. Glory flew under the wire three lengths ahead of Flightful.

Tears filled Cindy's eyes as the crowd cheered Ashleigh. Ashleigh waved proudly, standing high in her stirrups. She looked up into the stands and gave Cindy a thumbs-up.

"Way to go, Ashleigh and Glory!" Max cheered.

Cindy waved back at Ashleigh jubilantly. After that incredible ride, Ashleigh certainly deserved all the admiration and thanks the crowd was giving her. And Cindy knew that Glory had proved himself a champion, too. He was headed toward major stakes races in Saratoga—and after that, the Breeders' Cup!

JOANNA CAMPBELL was born and raised in Norwalk, Connecticut, and grew up loving horses. She eventually owned a horse of her own and took riding lessons for a number of years, specializing in jumping. She still rides when possible and has started her three-year-old granddaughter on lessons. In addition to publishing over twenty-five novels for young adults, she is the author of four adult novels. She has also sung and played piano professionally and owned an antique business. She now lives on the coast of Maine in Camden with her husband, Ian Bruce. She has two childern, Kimberly and Kenneth, and three grandchildren.

KAREN BENTLEY rode in English equitation and jumping classes as a child and in Western equitation and barrel-racing classes as a teenager. She has bred and raised Quarter Horses and, during a sojourn on the East Coast, owned a half-Thoroughbred jumper. She now owns a red roan registered Quarter Horse with some reining moves and lives in New Mexico. She has published nine novels for young adults.